MULBERRY BARK

A MULBERRY BARK BOOK

Published by

Mulberry Bark Publishing

Copyright © 2010 Michelle Cushing

PUBLISHER'S NOTE

This book is a work of fiction. Names, characters, places, and incidents either are products of the author's imagination or are used fictitiously. Any resemblance to actual events or locales or persons, living or dead or reincarnated, is entirely coincidental.

The character Travis Edwards first appeared in the novel *The Mask of Aubrey Clover* and is copyright © XT, the novel's author, and is used with permission.

For information contact Mulberry Bark Publishing.

http://www.mulberrybark.com

http://www.mulberrybark.com/michellecushing

ISBN: 978-0-9796935-5-7

Printed in the United States of America

MULBERRY BARK

*For the lovers, the poets, the magicians, the mystics ...
and my beloved, wherever and whoever you may be*

Also by Michelle Cushing

From a Vine
Faith Orion's Field

The blue sky does not fear the black
They are the same
Dawn and dusk

~Michelle Cushing, 2010

September 1926

Bess,

Love and kisses and lots of them, as always your husband until and after the curtain rings down on our lives, e'er to the crack of doom ...

Harry

Thunderstorms

Eric Pilot's belief in magic started as a little boy with the word buttermilk. Not something normally associated with anything mystical, but that word taught him a lesson about life and about love too. Death, he learned, was like a magic trick, even if it is a secret that only the magician and his assistant understand. The great magician Harry Houdini once said that magic was never a mystery to him; it came naturally, simply, as if he had done it all before, a past life maybe. Death – it was no different, just a simple sleight of hand trick. For some people it was like that. Eric was one of those people.

His mind was sharp as lightning, and he could spot a ruse like a detective on a case. As the passenger train rumbled through the Ozark Mountains in the early morning, Eric shuffled a deck of cards and admired the leaves turning red, yellow, and orange. He thought it was like magic – one minute brand new and green, the next amber and wilted, but still vibrant, beautiful. His parents and grandparents were orange leaves. Some day they would be green again. He believed this completely. Death, remember, a simple illusion.

His understanding of magic started on the day of his grandfather's funeral many years ago. Grandma Pilot had found Eric on her bed, tearing a thread from the quilt she had been perpetually knitting for him since his birth. The seven-year-old had resolved himself not to go to the funeral. Out of protest, you see, because Grandpa Pilot had lied. He had promised not to die. Yet he was dead. Feeling like a lost deck of playing cards stuck deep in the back of a drawer, Eric had sat on his grandparents' bed with no tears but with a flicker of rage in his eyes. If a tear had slipped out, no doubt it would have felt like melting wax. Outside it had been a cold winter, as it always was in Fairbanks, Alaska on his grandparents' ranch. Eric had looked at the trees, sickly sticks for branches, weighing heavy with ice, a blanket of snow as far as he could see. To him, it did not look like a fluffy, puffy playground to build a snowman. It just looked cold. Barren. Endless. Leading nowhere. Grandma Pilot, a sturdy but stick-thin woman with long gray hair in a ponytail, had leaned in the doorway watching him pull at that piece of thread from the blanket. It had various patches, mostly shades of green, but the one of a biplane to represent his last name was his favorite.

"You're going to pull that thread until you have a pile of loose yarn. You want that to happen?" she had said on that icy day, taking a seat beside him, patting his head.

"Grandpa lied." The words in his mouth were sticky, oozing like hot tar.

"He didn't lie, Eri," she had said, calling him by his nickname. For a long while, the kids at his new school thought his name was Harry since "Eri" sounded that way. "Come spring, those trees will have green leaves again," she had told him, pointing at the trees outside. "Remember what we talked about after your parents died?" Eric had looked into his grandmother's eyes, eyes of blue, not a cold blue like the way the sky looked on that freezing winter Alaskan day, but a soft blue like a baby's blanket, a crystal clear stream to carry away sorrow (and he had hoped it would not burden her, weigh her down with pain). Trusting, the rage within him subsided to a faint glimmer. She had gotten very close to him, whispered in his ear, "I'm going to tell you a secret, one that your grandfather and I share, and you'll know Grandpa Pilot did not lie."

What she had told Eric that day could be regarded by some as an old woman's silly wishful thinking, and what happened later as a mere coincidence, but it was the match that lit a different type of fire in young Eric that stayed with him forever. Not only did Eric lose his fear of death, but he gained a longing that was hard for a young child to grasp. On that day, his grandmother swore that Eric's eyes changed from pale brown to black as coal. His eyes became an endless night sky searching for a sun to light it, an eternal flame.

As a thirty-three-year-old man that same fire burned within him. It burned so hot, the believers say, that a strange flicker emanated from his gaze. Eric looked through the steam mist rising from the bottom of the train. Dawn. The sun looked like a great fire in the distance, warming the day, but a dark cloud hovered near it, promising rain up ahead. The cloud appeared endless but Eric could see the blue sky beyond it. A sun-fueled day. That was Eric's destination.

As if mystically held by an invisible barrier, two trains rested nose to nose on tracks side-by-side. The dark cloud that Eric had seen in the distance was now unmoving, unleashing torrents of water over the covered, outdoor, railway platform in the quiet, small town of Altus, Arkansas. The front headlights, like a giant eye on each train, flickered against the splatter of rain. The trains seemed to be staring at each other, as if they had driven all that way on a mission to meet one another. The scheduled moment of their meeting had arrived, and there they were, face to face, steam rising. But, the day looked gloomy, sullen. Gray. There was certainly no feel in the air of a great love about to blossom.

Through the fog, Eric walked, lost in his thoughts, and absentmindedly found a bench on the platform. He pulled out a book and waited for his connection. Eric didn't see the girl staring at him.

"Backpacker," Dawn Corner imagined, because Eric looked like he had been traveling awhile – faded black jeans with a hole in the knee, black T-shirt, lazy flop of brown hair covered by a tattered gray fedora with a black band. His battered knapsack was getting a little wet underneath the bench. He didn't seem to care, lost in his book, occasionally flipping a marshmallow from a Ziploc bag into his mouth. A green hand-stitched blanket, the one from his grandmother, covered his feet that were lackadaisically propped up on the bench. He leaned all the way back, using the armrest as a headrest, and held the book high above his head. It was an odd way to read, Dawn thought, with his arms up.

A loud thunderclap and Dawn jumped back, turning away from Eric. She tried to pretend it didn't frighten her but it did. Most things did. The lightning created a weird band of color, the sun trying to get out. It looked like the Northern Lights, the Aurora borealis, named after the Roman god of dawn. Just beyond the lights and the mountain in the distance, Dawn's mother was freshly buried. The dirt on her grave no doubt now a big hill of mud. And beyond the rolling hills in a deep valley, her father smoked a cigarette – he was rotting also, but in a barred jail cell. Her maternal grandfather, the one with the thick fingers calloused from picking grapes for wine, was buried near his wife in a family monument not far from their home. The vineyard Dawn grew up in had always been heavy like an anchor, resisting storm and swell, tying her in place. It would never fly away like Dorothy's house in the *Wizard of Oz*. Now, the home was adorned with a sign marked sold. Everything was buried. Everyone was dead.

As the two trains moved on to parts unknown, Dawn waited impatiently under the overhanging, her orange suitcase splattered with raindrops as water rushed down the grooves of the train tracks. The grooves looked like the irrigation tracks of their vineyard, if their winery had been made of steel, and to Dawn it had felt that cold. A leaf rushed by, headed down the tracks. As a child, Dawn would pick a grape, place it on a leaf, and let it float down the water trail. The grape got to escape. Now Dawn's tracks pointed in a new direction, she the porter controlling the breaks.

Antsy, Dawn checked her watch, checked the clock. Same time. She looked at her ticket, glanced at the platform number above her (D3). She was in the right place. It was futile to wish a constant such as time to bend and speed up. There were no magic words to change it. Faintly, she heard music (something about "Rosabelle") and turned around. Eric had one iPod headphone stuck in his ear, the other hung lazily across his shoulder. He too was checking his watch, an antique pocket watch that he casually stuck back in his pocket.

She tried to see the cover of his book, but she could only see the face of someone. Dawn took off her glasses, wiped away a waterdrop from the lens with the hem of her dress. She looked at Eric's book again. Probably a biography. She couldn't tell it was Houdini. If she had, she would have seen it as a funny coincidence and nothing more. See, Houdini is what lured Dawn to a job in Hot Springs. Her destination too. But Dawn didn't care about magic, the cruel trickery of it. She cared about escape, and the great magician was an expert at that.

Dawn was a master of illusions, as well. If one were to imagine Dawn's biography just by looking at her on that rain-soaked day, they would have seen a ray of sunshine in a darkened world. The dress she wore was pale orange lace, changing like a leaf from the hem to the neck to a faint yellow. With black hair cut into a bob, she wore black pumps and carried a 1920s-style beaded purse. Her skin pale. Her look old-fashioned. If one were to look a little closer, however, see the real face on the cover of her biography, they would see a cold damp heart. Dawn was like a factory-sealed book still in a plastic covering, no one ever allowed to peek inside at the pages, still on the shelf ... chosen by no one ... yet. In a few moments, Eric would see her, but he would see a faint glow in her eyes, a little ember that had been stomped, nearly put out, but wishing wanting to rage.

Dawn looked down the tracks again. Where was the train? She walked towards the ticket counter and passed Mademoiselle Danielle's Parisian Ice Cream. For a moment, she wondered how Parisian ice cream could be any different from regular ice cream. Either way, the ice cream sounded good, cold and sweet. Her stomach grumbled, but she walked timidly over to the ticket window instead. A man who looked like a stereotypical New York cab driver barely glanced up at her. Before she could speak, he said, "Look, lady, it's the storm. Train's comin'." Without a word, she walked back to the tracks and tripped over Eric's knapsack which he had just moved in preparation for the train's arrival.

Take a black piece of flint and strike it against steel and you'll get a spark. The meeting of Dawn and Eric was much like that, his eyes ignited like a piece of stone. In Eric's black eyes, Dawn thought she caught a glint of red-gold-then-orange like a fire blazing in a far-off mountain range. Just one flick and it was an inferno. Inside Dawn, the kindling flicked to life. Her cheeks went rosy, and a little flame made its way to the surface. She went warm as if the pilot light inside her had been lit. But, unlike the old cliché, for Dawn time did not stop when she looked into Eric's eyes. It sped up. Dawn's heart beat a little faster. The rain crashed against the pavement a little louder. And the train got to its destination a little bit quicker (with or without a magic word).

For Eric, time froze. Snap. Like a photograph preserved in time. Even his eyes did not blink as he looked up at her. His breath stopped momentarily. His fingers motionless on an unturned page.

Dawn certainly didn't know she loved him. To her, Eric was like a cloud. She could only pass through him, never hold him, never bring him home. Clouds dissipate, change, keep moving. They don't stay in the sky forever. Like all things in her life, nothing ever stayed, and yet nothing ever changed. She failed to realize, however, that clouds also turn to rain ... falling on her pale skin, wetting her hair, warming her lips, and stopping her dead in her tracks – a thundershower she never saw coming.

"Miss," the ticket counter man said, "there's your train. Right on time."

As if time were still out of sync with the rest of the world, Dawn glanced back, heard the whir of the approaching train, saw the headlight coming down the tracks. Something magical had just happened, but the world kept moving, oblivious. She went to the edge of the platform to wait. Her train. As it approached, windows zipping by before stopping, she felt the wind rush past her. It felt right. The train jerked to a halt in front of her. The doors opened, and the rain stopped as if to let her onboard, but she didn't step on, nor did she look up at the sky like the rest of the passengers who hesitated before getting off, expecting a downpour. Instead, Dawn looked back at the bench. Through the crowd, the hustle, the bustle, she saw him, shaking water off his knapsack, about to stand up. He slung the little blanket over his shoulder and walked toward the train. Their train. She turned back around, waited for all the passengers to disembark. As the crowd rushed to step off the train, and new passengers to get on, Eric bumped into Dawn, accidentally as if he hadn't seen her there. But he had. It didn't surprise Dawn that he missed her though. People usually did. Dawn was not the type of woman to stand out in a crowd. She was not beautiful. She was not ugly. She was just there. Like an entranceway. People passed through her. But not Eric. To him, she was solid. Like oak. He didn't know at this time that her bark was deeply scarred.

   With a faint smile and nod, Eric held out his hand for her to step onboard, gentlemanly. She felt him behind her, not close but she could smell his cologne. If she had to guess, she would say he smelled sweet like maple. Timidly, she glanced back, knowing he wasn't paying any-more attention to her. But he was.

   Red booth seats faced one another like on an old-fashioned train. Dawn found a spot and attempted to stuff her suitcase into the overhead bin. Being overfilled with other suitcases, her luggage barely fit, and she tipped back a step trying to maneuver it into place. This time it was she who bumped into Eric. He grabbed her luggage, easily popped it into the bin. He nodded again, another faint smile, and stuffed his knapsack next to her suitcase. As he rummaged around in his bag, Dawn quietly eased into the seat, believing she was still oblivious in his eyes and to those of everyone else on the train. Closer now, she could smell his cologne more clearly. He did not smell like maple syrup but a maple leaf. Green, earthy, but sweet, the way the vineyard smelled after the sun warmed a rainy day. With his arms raised, his T-shirt lifted up and exposed his stomach. A thin strip of hair ran from his navel to the button of his jeans. For politeness only, Dawn looked away. Eric threw his blanket onto the seat across from her, clamped the luggage bin closed, and sat down. Facing each other, she scooted closer to the window to sit diagonally from him (a straight line across – too much just then). Her eyes fluttered about, trying to ignore those eyes of his (but wanting to meet his gaze too). Being better at hiding curiosity, Eric put his bag of marshmallows on his lap and went back to his book. She could see it clearly now – the biography of Houdini. Somewhere deep in her gut, she felt a pang and did not know why. She closed her eyes, thinking she could stifle it, push it back down. She opened her eyes. The view from the window was blurred by condensation and she wiped it away. Through the mist rising from the bottom of the steaming train, she could make out a very dark cloud in the distance. To say it loomed, was a grave understatement. It made the storm clouds around them seem like dirty cotton balls. The formation was ominous. Not puffy, fluffy, or light. It was a rock – heavy, threatening, and very, very dark. She shivered.

"This will warm you up," Eric said, handing her his blanket. Masculine, but not too deep, his voice made her blush. She noticed the scar on Eric's wrist; he did not try to hide it. His hand was perfectly manicured. "Go on," he said, friendly. "You look cold."

Barely a smile, she took the blanket from him. For a few seconds (time seeming to play tricks on them again), they looked at one another like two people trying to remember the other's name, but her look had an air of distrust, his a look of compassion. She wrapped the blanket around her.

"Better?" he asked, noticing that her hand was on

the patch of the inkwell and quill, the last one his grandmother had stitched.

"Thank you," she said in a voice that was not soft-spoken, but quiet like someone wanting to speak up but afraid of being caught by the librarian.

Eric nodded, another faint smile, and stretched out, putting his feet up on the seat beside her. Quickly, she glanced down and noticed his shoes. Not what she expected. Shiny, looking brand new, and expensive. It didn't match the rest of his attire at all – a pair of black dress shoes with jeans and a T-shirt, just like a scar on a manicured hand. She rested her head on the cool window, keeping an eye on him as the train started to move. Secretly, she sniffed the blanket as she hugged it close to her, looking at all the embroidered patches, tracing the biplane.

The train's horn bellowed and Dawn let out a little shriek, being caught off guard. Eric glanced not at her, but out the window instead. Another faint smile rested on his face, but not at Dawn's little outburst. His eyes focused on the dark cloud. She focused, surreptitiously, on him with quick looks the way a person might continually glance at a celebrity in an airport while trying to remain nonchalant. A bead of sweat dripped down Dawn's temple, but she kept the blanket next to her. She liked the warm. Somewhere in her gut now she felt shame, like a sour gum drop that would not digest and pass. The sweet scent of Eric's blanket and his woodsy cologne settled in her stomach like a fine mist. Fog, she thought, looking outside, a heavy cloud sitting on the ground. The train rumbled through it, the mist opening, separating, and moving on.

Later, if rain could be like fire, the storm that descended upon that train in a heavy sheet was like an inferno, bringing with it drops of water that sounded like BBs shot out of a machine gun onto tin foil. To have heard it, one would have thought the roof were about to collapse.

Hail smashed into puddles, tapped at the windows, and ripped leaves from trees. But the little train rumbled on. Into a tunnel they went and everything went black.

Dawn watched Eric's eyes as he read. Very slowly his eyes moved, catching every word. He did not skim. Eric had pulled a reading light from his bag and clamped it to his book. He was the only thing vividly illuminated on the train. She was glad for the light and held his blanket closer still. Although the light did not move in a flicker across his pale skin, Eric's face looked luminous as if it were brightened with an oil lamp. The train was adorned with such lamps on the walls, but only for appearances. When she was a little girl, Dawn's childhood playhouse was an abandoned train caboose nestled far back in the woods of her home. She had used an old oil lamp to light it, kept her antique dolls there, and stowed away whenever she felt afraid, but that caboose had no tracks; it went nowhere.

A rickety creak-wobble-creak-wobble noise rolled into their train car. Flitting her eyes from passenger to passenger, a woman pushed a trolley down the aisle, following the illuminated track lighting on the floor and offering refreshments with a voice as sweet as the goodies on her cart. With a friendly flick of her wrist, she passed out treats and told the passengers that emergency power would be on soon. When she caught sight of Eric – his handsome face illuminated – she gazed at him as if he were a rare chocolate that she planned to keep all to herself, but Eric never looked up at her. The woman, not wanting to be slighted, imagined he was engrossed in his book, the look of concentration on his face, noticeable even with the brim of his hat casting a shadow on his face. Eric was concentrating, that was true, but he was secretly immersed in Dawn.

Dawn fumbled in her purse, looking for a dollar or

loose change. The weird feeling in her stomach was still there and she wanted to quell it. The emergency power kicked in and the car was filled with a lame dim yellow haze. Dawn pulled out her wallet – three hundreds, five twenties. She didn't want to break the bills for candy. She stuffed the envelope back into her purse, resigning herself to suffering. Before she could lift her head, a bag of marsh-mallows were held out to her. Giving her no time to refuse, Eric placed the sweets on her lap with a quick nod.

"You looked like you could use something sweet," he said, putting his feet firmly on the ground. He put his book aside and opened a package of licorice-flavored Jack 9 gum from his pocket. The remembered-taste of licorice made her blush, the same pit of shame stirring in her gut. She thanked him with a cautious smile. Eric tipped his hat, then took it off, placing it on his knee. He ran his hand through his thick hair.

She pushed his blanket aside and took out a marsh-mallow slowly as if it were a snake that might bite her back.

"Marshmallows look like little clouds," he said.

She gently pressed a marshmallow with her thumb and index finger. It bulged out. She looked at it for a seconds then ate it. Loved the sweet. The puffiness. The way it melted but not really and went down in one sweet mo-tion.

"What's in Hot Springs for you?" he asked.

"A job," she replied. Her Southern voice was like molasses, slow, sweet, a little bitter.

Eric waited, chewed his gum slowly, expecting her to continue. "What kind of job?"

"At a museum's library. I'm an archivist. I pre-serve, restore, and catalog old records, documents." Talk-ing about her job was always easy. Dawn spoke like a telegraph machine, clicking out the words without feeling, just fact.

"You like things in order," Eric said, as if pondering a decision and coming to a conclusion for her, but he was right. "Have you ever been to Hot Springs before?"

Yes, the first time she ever tasted licorice. Most of the trip was a vague memory; she had only been three years old and was visiting her paternal grandmother, a very poor woman who lived in a trailer with a hole rotting so deeply in the living room that the ground outside could be seen through it. She was dead now too, but on that day she had taken Dawn to see a movie. Dawn did not remember the film but had a clear image of being at the concession stand and seeing that jar filled with black licorice sticks. "Can you eated those twigs?" she had asked back then. And because her mother never let her have much candy, her paternal grandmother out of spite for Dawn's mother, not real affection for Dawn, bought her five sticks (counting all the loose change from the bottom of her purse to pay for the extra treats). Dawn loved the way the candy bent without breaking, and she had never tasted anything so sweet. Even to this day, Dawn thought the branches of leafless trees looked like licorice.

Outside now, as the train rolled on, the storm swelling, Dawn could see no trees. The train jolted, popping open the window slightly. Cool air and misty raindrops trickled inside and kissed her face. She watched Eric chew slowly – he savored the gum with his mouth in the same way he read every word of a book.

"My father's mother used to live in Hot Springs," she said in answer to Eric's question. "I used to visit her when I was really small before she died."

"Is that why you want to work there?"

"No. I was just a baby. I don't even remember anything about Hot Springs." She also did not remember much more about that grandmother, other than her drafty trailer being warmer than her comfortable home in Altus.

Eric nodded his head, contemplating her words as if they were sentences he had written. Dawn looked away. So dark outside. He popped his gum – CRACK – Dawn looked him in the eye, and the lights popped on in the train. "Magic!" he said with a laugh.

With the bright lights back on, people got up and started to move about the cabin. Cautiously and with a cavalier attitude, a little girl with curly hair walked past Eric and Dawn as if afraid of spilling a too-filled drink, but she carried no such cup. Tip-toeing, arms outstretched like a tight-rope walker, she went up to a woman with blond hair, who was sitting not far from them.

"Shake me. I'm magic," the little girl exclaimed with a cool air, almost mocking, but hoping the woman would respond.

As if the child had spoke to Eric instead, he looked at her, caught off guard as if someone had yelled "Fire!" His eyes widened, and Eric watched the little girl closely. Playfully, the woman shook the child until coins fell from the ringlets in the girl's hair. One coin rolled down the aisle; Eric stuck out a foot and stepped on it, stopping it from going any farther. The girl strolled over to pick it up.

"Wild," Eric said to her.

The girl explained, "I put some dollars in the coin machine and got all these quarters. I put them in my hair."

"I dig it."

"Dig it like a gravedigger," the kid said, cool-like, and sauntered back to the woman, picking up the coins. "Look at all this moolah!"

Quietly, Eric chuckled as if he finally caught the punch line to a joke. He looked at Dawn, who was only slightly amused in a curious sort of way.

"Magic," Eric said, tapping his book, but Dawn turned to the rain outside.

She ate the last marshmallow without having realized she had finished the bag. "I'm sorry. I didn't mean to eat all of them."

Eric shrugged. "Little clouds." He pointed outside to the rain clouds. "I can get you some of those, although they tend to shrink on the journey from the sky."

"What?"

The window was still slightly open, raindrops kept landing on her. Eric reached over, pulled the window all the way down, and stuck his hand outside. The rest of the passengers looked at him suspiciously. Dawn leaned far back, pulled his blanket around her again. He shut the window, his right palm balled into a fist, and stuck it out at her, asking her to hold out her hand. When she did, he dropped several marshmallows into her palm.

"How'd you do that?"

"Magic."

In his dark eyes, she saw that red-gold-then-orange flicker again. She shivered but she was not cold.

"Still cold?" he asked.

"A little. Aren't you?" She held his blanket out to him. "You can have your blanket – "

"No, keep it. I'm fine. I'm Alaskan. This isn't cold to me."

"You traveled here all the way from Alaska?" she asked, eating the marshmallows.

Eric liked the surprised look on her face but he did not laugh or even grin. "I didn't travel from Alaska per se. I've been on the road a lot this year. I was in Kansas City, then St. Louis, then Fayetteville. I was born in Anchorage, raised in Fairbanks. In the interior. Northern Lights and all that jazz. Coca-Cola polar bears."

She snorted a little laugh and quickly covered her mouth. Heaven opened up – a little more and the rain might have stopped outside.

"They're very pesky," he said of the polar bears

from the soda commercials. "Always wanting to drink your Coke." He watched her closely.

Dawn covered her face, so he wouldn't see how much she wanted to laugh again, but he knew. She was transforming. The flicker in his eyes – red-gold-then-orange – stronger than ever. A bead of sweat rolled down his cheek. She rubbed his blanket – Eric still looking at her – static electricity shocked her, sending a momentary arc between her fingers that she was sure only she glimpsed. A lightning bolt cut across the sky like a gold knife cutting the dark sky in two. She pulled her knees up to her chest and wrapped the blanket around her. "It's just rain," he said softly. "It won't hurt you." Through the window, they both saw the gray cloud mixing with black smoke. In the distance, something was burning ... even in the pouring rain.

Transformation

Eric's antique pocket watch had stopped at 1:26 p.m. He shook it and tried to wind it with the winding key, but it would not tick. He stuffed it back in his pants pocket, paid the cab driver, and stepped into the sunshine streaming between the dark clouds. Hopping over a puddle, Eric looked up at the grand Arlington Hotel with its white-washed walls and giant twin towers surrounded by trees with fall foliage. He wasn't sure what time it was. Stepping inside the lobby was like entering a different world and for a moment Eric saw it, the way he always saw things other people did not. In his mind, the place was filled with women in cloché hats with bobbed hair, some twirling flapper beads. He imagined that in a far right corner a jazz band played, while in the opposite corner Al Capone sat with a group of cohorts, talking in secret and smoking a cigar. As he looked around the lobby, his fantasy continued, conjuring a group of men just back from an expedition of Egypt, discussing Howard Carter's discovery of King Tutankhamun's tomb. Eric envisaged people walking past, laughing about a Harold Lloyd film, over-thinking surrealist art, or discussing the art deco design of the hotel. Of course, in reality, businessmen and businesswomen talked on cell phones, hotel staff lugged baggage, and tourists lounged in T-shirts and jeans. It didn't matter.

Anything from another time, Eric loved it and that is how he saw it. Even now, he had a 1930 Duesenberg at his home in Alaska, listened to records on a mahogany Victor V model Victrola, and wrote with an antique fountain pen that once belonged to Sir Arthur Conan Doyle. When Eric was a little boy he kept all of his favorite things in a 1920s-style traveling trunk. It wasn't really from the 1920s, but one made to look old-fashioned, sold at a discount store for ten dollars. Inside, Eric had kept his grandfather's deck of cards, some of his parents' ballroom dancing trophies, his blanket (in the summer), a photo of silent film star Glenda Goodall (whom he had a crush on), his Senor Captain Magic action figure, and a model airplane with one of the wings accidentally glued on upside down. He also kept his journals. After Eric's eyes went from brown to black with a spark of something yet unknown to him – when he became a believer in magic – he starting writing poetry. Even before death took up residence in his life, Eric had always loved words, spelling being his favorite subject in school. Words could be defined, arranged, and rearranged like building blocks. Whenever someone said a word he did not know, he had always looked up at them and said, "Spell and define," no doubt mimicking the voice of his teacher. His favorite word had always been "transformation." It had been on his spelling test the day his parents had died. The bigger the word, the smarter the little boy felt. Such a word sounded big and felt good coming out of his mouth. He let words roll off his tongue, wrote them over and over to make sure he formed each letter just right. When his parents died, to his vocabulary, he added the words "death" and "collision" –

words that were technically smaller than "transformation" because they had fewer letters, but they had bigger meaning.

But "transformation" had remained one of his favorite words. Partly because it was the first "big" word he had learned to spell, but mostly he liked the meaning. A word, whose definition meant becoming something else. That's how his grandmother had explained death to him. "That's all death is, Eri. Just a change. Like putting on a new pair of boots because the other ones wore out," she had said.

Such abstract things were never hard for Eric to grasp, and eventually, he filled far too many notebooks of poetry, short stories, and thoughts to keep inside one small trunk. Grandma Pilot had encouraged his love of the written word, but his parents were the catalyst for his love of the old-fashioned. It was as if they had popped into existence like time travelers stepping from one century to the next, enjoying the modern but refusing to give up a long-gone era. As champion ballroom dancers, they always had old-timey music playing, everything from waltzes to Benny Goodman and Tommy Dorsey. His mother, Harmony, collected antique dishes; his father, Everett, renovated classic cars. Both dressed to the nines when they went out dancing, their shoes always gleaming, perfectly polished with a gentle click as they walked, a rhythmic tappity tap when they danced. So, while Eric grew up with all the comforts of a modern well-fed warm life, he had something most children did not, the gentle hum of something from the past calling to him softly like a mother calling him to supper.

All of this charmed him, cultivated him like a plant, but it was the way his parents loved, the same way his grandparents loved, that taught him how to be a romantic. Whenever little Eric had caught his mother and father holding hands or kissing gently, they never shooed him away. To see his parents in love was as natural as watching her bake a batch of cookies, a warm part of life. No shame or guilt involved, just happiness. So, therefore, Eric himself never had to be transformed into a romantic. He was born in a soup of gentle, genuine, good.

Dawn could smell sage and celery stewing. A billow of smoke came from her landlord's little house, one that looked much like a dollhouse from a Grimm Fairytale with pink shutters, flower boxes, and a chimney that was striped like a black-and-white candy cane. The chimney puffed out the smoke in one continuous stream like a cigarette left in an ashtray, snaking up to the sky, a sky that was still dark. The sunlight breaking through the clouds slowly transformed the landscape from gray to color.

"A pretty lil' rainbow up ahead. You see it, love?" asked her British landlord, Mrs. Crumper, who spoke rapidly, but not unpleasantly, like the sound of windshield wipers on a rainy day. Dawn did not actually look for the rainbow but nodded anyway. "So good to have some rain," Mrs. Crumper said as she opened the front door of the apartment complex, which was separated from the landlady's home by a small, well-tended garden of mums and apple trees, which had ripe fruit but blooms too. "I'm making a pot of soup. Come have some with me when you get settled. It'll warm you up, love. Fall weather, beautiful as it is, brings a chill too," Mrs. Crumper said.

Up the worn stairs they went to the third and last floor. The apartment complex was old, but it had a nice patina to it. Dawn had fallen in love with the little apartment on Rahner Street when she had inspected it soon after her mother had died. Inside, the chipped paint was green, the floor creaked, and the curtains were yellowed-lace. There was only a small kitchen attached to a living room. No dining room to speak of and one bedroom and bathroom.

Her new landlord had a nice patina to her, as well. With wild red hair, the sixty-year-old looked like a Cyndi Lauper video reject. There was a gargoyle stitched onto the front of her apron, and she wore far too much dark lipstick (which she told Dawn was called Sexy Midnight). She reminded Dawn of Mrs. Garrett from the *Facts of Life* if Mrs. G had been hot-to-trot.

"I love autumn," the landlady rambled on. "Do you like fall? I love how it transforms everything, gets our little neighborhood ready for winter."

Dawn only nodded.

"Some of your things arrived this morning," Mrs. Crumper said, handing Dawn a little gold key that looked antique. It glinted in the poorly lit hallway and Dawn shivered. Dawn quickly opened the apartment door.

"I moved the boxes into the corners so you could move about more easily," Mrs. Crumper said as they went inside.

"The rest of my bags and furniture should arrive soon," Dawn told her.

"Should you be out, me and Mitch are always here to accept deliveries, love" she said, referring to her black-and-white Boston Terrier, who at that moment was in the garden peeing on a ceramic gnome. Instinctively, Mrs. Crumper peeked out the window, made a slight scoff at the sight, and said while tapping on the window, "That dog's always peeing on me Leon." She looked at Dawn. "Leon the Gnome guards the premises."

Dawn raised an eyebrow and looked outside. Her landlady was crazy. But she ignored this ... the sky so dark ... but slowly transforming.

"I love that dog, but he doesn't mind worth a damn." She shook her fist as if the dog could see her. Nosily, Mrs. Crumper opened the flap on one of the boxes, which had already been opened and resealed. "Be happy to help unpack, if you need it." Dawn shook her head. "I've never seen so many pretty ceramic dolls," Mrs. Crumper said, peeking inside one of the boxes.

"I've collected them since childhood."

She more than collected. She used to steal them. The abandoned train caboose in the woods behind her childhood home had been filled with stolen dolls. She was not a deceptive girl, she never wanted to steal, but Dawn could not ask for what she really wanted. While Eric grew up in a warm soup, Dawn was raised in a cold broth. Her mother, Bobby Jane Corner (B.J. for short), was suppose to have been born a boy, the heir to the family business, Corner Wine. She had the voice of a woman but the tincture of a man, something darker, deeper than her little pursed lips should have held. B.J. was brusque in every manner, ordering Dawn, the household staff, and vineyard employees around like soldiers. B.J. clunked about their home in harsh suits of dark-colored linen, kept her hair very short, and read the *Wall Street Journal* every night in a leather office chair (no rolling wheels, stoic, stuck in place). Dawn always thought her mother looked like a small Frenchman and wished she could paint a moustache on her to make it more true.

While Dawn always had plenty of cash and every modern gadget, the idea of playing with dolls was out of the question. B.J. thought dolls were useless items and would not give Dawn a head start as the heir to Corner Wine, so Dawn kept her back straightened (it makes you look more imposing, her mother said) and did what she was told. Always what she was told ... but she really liked the dolls. Stealing was the only option, because her mother made Dawn account for every purchase with a receipt. It was a "business practice," B.J. had said, and Dawn should get used to it. Each penny was accounted for in a ledger, her allowance carefully controlled, rising and falling according to current interest rates, accounting for inflation and such.

Covertly, Dawn had scoured the town, stealing from flea markets, antique shops, and neighbors. She stashed the dolls away from her mother's squinting ledger-filled eyes. While Dawn was finally far away from the constant attention of her dead mother, those harsh teachings forced her into a crack that was too small for her to fit. Her mind became like a bubbling pot of stew, so many thoughts concealed with a lid that lifted and fell with each bubble, small pieces seeping out into her consciousness. As best as she could, Dawn clamped the lid tightly on her thoughts, sealing them like a pressure cooker.

Boom! Lightning hit a transformer, sending sparks into the air.

"Fireworks!" Mrs. Crumper exclaimed, unfazed. The lights in the apartment flickered. She ignored it and continued inspecting Dawn's dolls. "This one looks like a gothic Snow White," Mrs. Crumper said, picking up the only doll Dawn had never stolen. Her first. One that was given to her. Given to her by a man her mother used to love. It had been a wintery Christmas morning, like something in a child's holiday cartoon, absolutely perfect – a glass of milk and cookies left for Santa now all consumed, star atop the Christmas tree still lit from the night before, and the softest patch of snow on the ground, still falling gently. The scent of celery and sage wafting from the kitchen. And there had been the ceramic doll. Up on the mantel as if Santa had left it there above her stocking. She didn't ask how he knew about her secret wish (he just knew, just like Santa, and that was enough). Before her mother could say a word, he scooted Dawn out of the house, and she carried the doll like a trophy to her little train caboose, placed it on a handmade shelf. Safe. It was perfect, beautiful, loved, belonging on a shelf. But the doll in Mrs. Crumper's hand had ratty, short-cropped hair, frayed dress, and scratched nail polish. It once had ringlets of black hair with a beaded black dress, wide-brimmed hat, and red fingernails. That was before the lock. That was before he solidified everything her mother had ever told her.

So while Eric's eyes shifted from brown to black, Dawn's eyes remained a dull pale brown. That was about to change though. That girl, who Eric had described in his journal during the cab ride to the hotel as "a little wisp of smoke seeping out of a corner," was indeed transforming, once barely a flicker, now ignited and about to rage. Fireworks.

A fireplace crackled and a grandfather clock swung back and forth, tick tock, returning, mesmerizing, hypnotizing. "Room 1926," said the hotel front desk clerk to Eric. Her voice had a wilted stammer like a phonograph skipping and slowing down at the same time. She stared into Eric's dark eyes like a bee eyeing the pollen-lined stamen of a flower. Consummation. That's all women wanted from him. That honey, that sweetness. Those dark eyes of his – the flicker of the red-gold-then-orange – made women open and wait, pick me like a unique flower swaying in a breeze filled with roses, tulips, and dandelions. My nectar is sweetest, they all seem to say. He unconsciously ignited women so warmly that they almost always started to sweat, their faces flushed, a little drop of dew on a petal in morning. The same effect was happening to the hotel clerk. A little bead of sweat dripped slowly between the woman's breasts, her eyes not moving from his face.

Clang! The clock chimed and the woman shuddered as if she had been awoken by a stranger after falling asleep in public. Politely, Eric smiled, took his key, and started to walk off. She busied herself with tasks, shuffling paper, arranging a pencil next to a notepad. With a shaking hand, she called him back, hoping. She handed him a tourist brochure, the "fun things to do" in Hot Springs. Maybe somewhere in his thoughts she would be one of them. She would not, because while Eric's passions were a caldera of lava and his thoughts were amorous, his intentions were singular, directed at the one.

The clerk pointed to the lobby, genteelly crossed her legs, and said, "The elevators are to your right, past the fountain. Enjoy your time here, Mr. Pilot." Her voice sounded sad.

The fountain was ornate and poured hot spring water into the lobby. Eric let his hand rest in the hot water for a moment. His hand flushed. For a brief moment more, Eric admired his surroundings, looked at the painting by Efram T. Corbet, an artist he admired and knew. The painting was of a fall weather tree with a man and woman underneath it. There were little triangle designs on the hotel wallpaper, orange and green, almost mixing with the colors in the painting, but the painting had a giant splosh of red in the corner – the sun ... and it burned bright.

When he reached his suite, Eric did not insert the key. He put his ear to the door like a criminal cracking a safe and tapped three times near the lock. The door popped open. Such were things with Eric. He made magical seem easy. Never needed a key.

His things – two authentic 1920s traveling trunks – had already been brought to his room. A chilled bottle of red Corner Wine, courtesy of the hotel manager, waited for him by the window. He had no clue who once owned the very grapes that made the wine. When Dawn and Eric had parted on the train, she had darted away so quickly, but through the crowd, she had looked back, spotted him like a bulls-eye, and he had waved, but somehow he knew that it was not goodbye.

Eric looked outside; an angry little cloud hovered several blocks away. A little fever went up his spine like a snake, resided coiled in his mind. He rubbed his temples, poured himself a glass of wine (was it sour?), and watched a man and woman walk side-by-side down the sidewalk. It was hard to say, Eric always thought, if two people were in love in today's day and age. No one held hands anymore, or kissed in public. There were no more shy winks, or tips of hats. Those behaviors were all antiques, not even for sale at a flea market. Romance (or was it merely sex now?), like a box of fast food French fries, was convenient and made everyone forget the joy in preparing real food.

His stomach rumbled, and he ordered a sumptuous lunch – roasted chicken, cornbread dressing, and mashed potatoes. He ate it with the wine, but it did not relax him. He went to the bedroom, kicked off his shoes, and fell onto his back on the bed. Anxious, that's what he was, and he could not sleep. Eric took a long shower then went back to the living room. He lit a fire in the fireplace and poked at the logs. He wasn't cold; it just felt right. A shadow rolled over the room, slowly darkening it as if someone had gently dropped a blanket over a bed. Eric flipped on the lights and looked outside again. The clouds had shoved the sunlight into a corner. The gray sky was making the window-pane reflect like a mirror.

A honeybee crawled up the window in a hurry. In a corner in a small crack in the windowsill was a red flower. "Ah, I see what you're after," Eric said, as if the insect could hear. "How'd you find that flower way up here?" He tapped at the glass, but the bee ignored him, collected the nectar, and flew away. "I could go for something sweet too." He called room service again, ordered a slice of apple pie, and sat down on the sofa. As he waited for his dessert, he looked at the splosh of red in the corner of the window, that little flower growing alone on the top floor of the hotel, and marveled at how a bee had found it.

Something popped in the fireplace, and Eric became mesmerized by the flames. He watched the logs slowly change to ash. Transformation ... and it reminded him ...

Eric went straight to his knapsack and found his journal. With his antique fountain pen, Eric sat on the sofa and hurriedly finished his thoughts about Dawn. "That girl was like a little wisp of smoke seeping out of a corner," he had already written. "One bit of friction and she ignited before me," he added quickly, his writing chicken scratch. "She saw me, burning and waiting." Then he added a little note to himself in parenthesis – "Does that sound corny?" He continued, slowed, his pen making slight scraping noises as he wrote, "What a curious girl. She wasn't shy per se, no not that really, in as much afraid. Yes, a girl in a corner, that's what she was for sure. I've never met one like her. Who is this frightened girl with bright face covered in night?"

Night

The clock said 1:26 a.m. It was raining again, storming, and Dawn huddled in the covers, watching the streaks of lightning in the sky through the window, waiting for the thunder that follows a few seconds later. Restless, she headed for the kitchen and flipped on every light in the apartment. She needed light. On the counter was the empty marshmallow bag that Eric had given her. It sat there among other bits of clutter from her suitcase and purse. She picked it up, tried to drop it in the trash, but static cling had taken full control of the package. It stuck to Dawn's hand, rolled around her fingers as she vigorously flicked it off. Gingerly, as if oblivious to her assault, it floated in the air and sailed down to her feet. She grabbed it, crumpled it, and dropped it in the trash with a gentle thud. In response, a bolt of lightning sent a flash of bright light into the room. Her shadow flickered before her like a ghost. Seeing it gave Dawn that feeling that anyone gets when looking in a mirror and having that tiny glimpse of self-realization. It made Dawn quickly look away. She opened the refrigerator; Mrs. Crumper had kindly stocked it

with a few necessities as a "courtesy on move-in day."
Milk, bacon, eggs, cheese. Lettuce and tomatoes in the
crisper. A loaf of bread and tray of homemade pumpkin-
spiced muffins on the counter. Dawn ate a muffin. She
wanted two, maybe even three or four, and was having
trouble deciding against it. One time she had eaten an entire bag of cookies in one sitting. Three bars of the choco-
late-and-peanut Mr. Goodyum at once. An entire box of
Krispy Kreme doughnuts one morning (that had been a
record). This usually happened when she was anxious (and
only when she was alone). Dawn picked up another muffin, remembered having made pumpkin bread once for
Thanksgiving. Her mother had just bought a state-of-the-
art oven that looked like black marble. Dawn had been
anxious to cook something of her own, so she made the
bread with a layer of marshmallow cream, but the oven had
a faulty pilot light, filling the kitchen with toxic gas. The
scene had looked like something from a cartoon with
everyone rushing around to air out the room. Her mother
had not found it funny at all. Another annoyance. And
Dawn's pumpkin bread was thrown out. Dawn wished she
had some marshmallows now. The little clouds. That's
what Eric had called them. A warm feeling in her stomach
... safe in her apartment in the night, even with the whipping wind outside, she let herself think – he was handsome.

She ate the second muffin and went to the bathroom, looked at her reflection in the mirror, not seeing the
girl she felt like inside. Dawn could only see the reflection
everyone else saw – thin lips, small brown eyes, and pudgy
nose, not a supermodel, not even an average-rate model.
No model at all. Just a girl. A girl who at age thirty should
have thought of herself as a woman.

She was born a skinny, near-sighted girl with a
piece of hair that constantly jutted out to the side like a
duck tail. The strange tuft was the favorite taunt of school-

mate Luanne Mixen, who had flaxen hair with two curls that dropped seductively beside each cheek. Luanne's voice, even in high school when she was the prettiest, most popular of girls, was that of a boy whose voice never changed. Not sweet like honey and without the same hue as molasses. No, it was sugared water. Unable to stomach. But the boys lapped it up like greedy pigs, and Dawn tried to keep that nasty bit of scraggily hair in place. It didn't matter, her mother had said. She was a weird-looking kid and boys only liked pretty girls which was a blessing be-cause they only caused heartache. See, B.J. Corner's soul was like clabbered oil in a very old car. It started out fine, smooth, but it was never cared for or maintained properly. She had her own parents to blame, her own parents to hate, and that is a story for another day. But once, and only once, Dawn saw her mother shine like new.

His name was Bale Howard and B.J. hired him to help run the vineyard. Dawn's first glimpse of him, as the four-year-old ran through the house to hide something in her train car, was like looking up at a giant. He was tall and sturdy as a walnut tree. He looked like the Brawny paper towel man, and he had smiled back down at little Dawn. When he had held out his arms, she jumped right in. Dawn had never had a man in her life, her father in jail, one grandfather merely a memory of cruel calloused hands, the other grandfather no memory at all. But Bale doted on Dawn, and she loved that his arms were soft and strong and he smelled like cotton, laundry fresh from the dryer. He kept a padlock hooked in a belt loop, he had told Dawn, for fun. Every morning when he came to work at the Corner Vineyard, he scooped up Dawn and carried the little girl outside, explaining to her when a grape was ripe, when it was rotted to the core. She had felt the grapes, tested to see if they were mushy, looked to see a dark spot inside. She had loved him, as had her mother. Neither saw his dark spot inside. She watched her mother transform from thorn to petal in only a few short weeks.

Far away in Alaska, little Eric had just learned to spell the word "transformation." He was about to learn the word "collision" and soon that the word "buttermilk" could be magical. Before that would happen, Dawn learned something too. "Men are like leaves, Dawn," her mother had explained. "They all turn brown eventually." She had said this to Dawn with a big bruise on her cheek. She didn't have to explain it. Dawn saw it happen. The wind had been atrocious, knocking over a small Japanese maple in the front yard, but Bale had thrown B.J. across the porch with more force than any wind. Those same hands that had gently picked a grape had also pulled her mother's hair. "You get inside or you're next, little girl!" he had yelled at Dawn. Stepping backward into the house, she had closed the front screen door, heard her mother yell, "Don't touch my daughter." More slapping, more tumbling, and so on and so forth until the police were called and Bale never came back again. That night Dawn had run to the caboose, saw Bale's padlock on the door. Her things would remain trapped like blood in veins for three long years until she read a children's biography about Houdini. Being inspired by the great escape artist (and never paying much attention to the love story inside), she pried the padlock open using a logical mathematical algorithm, not needing the combination numbers. Had someone seen this little girl doing such a thing, they would have declared her a genius with either a bright future or one of crime like her father. Once inside the train car again, with dull scissors – the snubbed ones for children that are only meant to cut construction paper – she cut the hair of the doll Bale had given her, tore at the dress, and etched off the nail polish. One slip of the scissors and a deep gash slashed across her arm. She didn't cry. She smelled the wound. Tasted it. While B.J.'s insides hardened even more, Dawn's insides turned to goo and when it felt too heavy, too thick, too much, she let it ease out with a pin-prick, a needle jab, or knife gnash. But she could never throw that little doll away. She wouldn't let anyone take that from her.

Hearing the wind howl outside now, the lights in the apartment flickering, no caboose to escape to, Dawn took a needle from her makeup bag and became mesmerized by the shiny metal, glinting by the light of the fluorescent bulb. She dipped the needle into a bottle of rubbing alcohol, blew on it to dry. Sinking to the floor, she poked the fleshy part of her palm until a drop of blood curdled out. She realized this form of catharsis was unacceptable. It was a weird irony, Dawn always thought, punishing oneself with something shameful for feeling or doing something shameful – like spanking a child for getting into a fist fight. She had only gotten caught once. It had started with a boy.

His name was Harry. There he had sat every day at lunch in the art room with his wavy black hair, a little piece that fell over his eyes which he rarely bothered to move. He had long slender fingers, coffee-colored skin, and large dark eyes that he often squinted because he needed to wear glasses. His lack of eyesight did not hinder his paintings, and Dawn admired each one, because they were always on display in the high school hallways like a museum for their most-likely-to-succeed student. He was cool, rebellious, and smelled like pancake batter. She liked to make pancakes nearly every morning so she too would have that aroma.

Working on the yearbook staff gave her an advantage, she saw every photo of him that came in for possible publication, and she stole or copied as many as she could, keeping them in a little folder in her train car. A few she kept beside her bed in a folder marked "science" so her mother wouldn't know the difference. At night she looked at each one, daydreamed about their wedding, what his kisses would feel like. If he held her hand, would he entwine his fingers or just clasp palms? If they went to the prom, would he buy her a corsage? All these daydreams in the night, until one day she had gathered the courage, found an excuse actually, to talk to him.

"Can I borrow an X-Acto knife?" she had asked, voice sounding like a nervous Huckleberry Hound. "For the yearbook staff. Ours are dull." He had pointed one out, but never looked at her. The very next day, Dawn felt him behind her at the lockers, his arm slung up against one, reclining, his hand dangling just above her head. Shyly, she had turned around. Looked up at him. His lips were perfect, barely open with a smile.

"Want a candy bar?" he had asked, the flippant voice of a teenage boy with misguided confidence. She nodded. But it was not an offer; it was a sales pitch. The art class needed money for a field trip and were selling candy bars. She bought three. The girl on the other side of her locker one-upped her and bought four, but Dawn didn't care. She took the candy home, ate two, and saved the other.

He returned soon after with another offer. Would she help with his leaf collection for science class? In the park near the playground, he drew sketches (but not of Dawn), while she reached up to the highest branches, hoping her skirt would raise, show a little seductive leg. On her tip-toes, she took the bright green leaves, especially the pointed maple ones. She liked those best, the way they smelled, the shape. Harry kept telling her, pointing to the ground, to take the brown ones.

"You can't save those. They're already dead," she had explained. He merely shrugged in a cool-boy nonchalant manner. He had kept pointing at them anyway. "You can't mount those. They're too brittle. They'll break," she had said, not exasperated at all, gently explaining again.

The young boy, they were both only sixteen, put down his sketch pad, backed her up against the tree, and kissed her. The first. The only. Nothing in her girlish fantasies prepared her for the licorice taste of his mouth (where had that come from?), the soft (not hard) bulge in his pants against her stomach, or the way his fingers dug into her neck leaving little marks. As he pulled away, and she had felt suspended for a moment as if the tree's bark had hold of her, Harry made a lewd joke about the spiky gum balls on the ground being the tree's testicles. Then he picked up a brown leaf, crushed it in his hand, making what looked like cereal flakes, and said, "Pick the brown ones. I like the way they crumple in my hand." She picked every one, knowing the project would get a C- at best. When she finished collecting leaves, Dawn had sat on a swing, waiting for him. Finally, he came over, took both ropes in his hand, stood above her and leaned down for a kiss. This time she was literally suspended in mid-air for a moment. But he did not kiss her. He said, "Now I have to go pee, honey." Harry packed up his things and headed in the other direction just as she heard the honk of her mother's car horn.

Once in the car, her mother had asked, "Did you kiss that boy?"

"No, we were just collecting leaves."

"He smokes." Her mother had grabbed her, sniffed her breath. "Licorice," B.J. had said, satisfied that Dawn had not kissed him, because she knew Dawn liked licorice. The thrill of getting away with it would be short-lived.

"I don't care about that frilly little fruitcake," were the first words she had heard the next day at school. It was by accident. Harry walked past her, right past as if she were a locker in the row, hand in hand with Luanne Mixen. "I don't care what anyone saw. I only used her to collect leaves. I'm failing science, babe. She's smart, you know. Real smart." And they walked on by ... never seeing her. Actually no one saw her that day accept her mother, who was notified that Dawn was absent (she never missed class). Dawn had ran home, snuck in through the window, destroyed the leaf collection, and inflicted twelve pinpricks into her palm. When her mother had seen the blood from a dozen needle jabs, she sent Dawn to sit in a corner like a child. After Dawn had been there an hour, the vineyard staff and household employees ignoring her like furniture, B.J. had bandaged her hand. It almost felt loving. "Don't do that again," she had told her, and Dawn never really knew if she meant the needle jabs or the school skipping.

In her caboose now, the property's new owner was no doubt finding that bar of candy Harry had sold her (rotted to dust), the X-Acto knife, and his yearbook pictures – all tucked inside a little box. It would be trashed, of course, which is where it belonged. But, the taste of licorice, like the doll Bale had given her, would not be discarded. She still liked it. No one would take that away from her. It reminded her of rebellion, of secrets, and even if she did not admit it to herself, it reminded her of love, albeit skewed.

On the floor of her new bathroom, those feelings for Harry were long gone, but the scars he inflicted were visible. Dawn stared at the bubble of blood. It spread out like an oval on her hand like an eye looking up at her, the same sickening way her mother had looked down at her that day many years ago. Seeing the blood reminded Dawn of something else, and she got up to change a tampon. She used tampons, not pads, because they slowly poked away at her virginity. The cycle was over, and she discarded the tampon in the trash. Unlike most women, Dawn liked having her period. It reminded her that she was normal.

But Dawn was far from normal. Her feelings when pushed, rushed out like fire ants attacking from an ant hill.

Her understanding of these feelings were crumpled and crushed like a balled up piece of paper. Eric would soon find this out. Growing up next to a warm fireplace – protected from the cold outside – Eric knew nothing of mean men who padlocked little girl's playhouses or women who sat their teenage daughters in corners. He only knew about love and magic. And since his heart was filled with such kindness, such genuine feeling, had he seen Dawn at this moment, cold and cuddled in a corner on the bathroom floor, sleeping with a blood-stained hand in the night, he would not have pitied her or wept or been disturbed. He would have lifted her up with hands that were too soft to be a man's hands, and he would have lit a fire to share. Which is what he would soon do. Morning on its way, that was guaranteed.

Morning

Aside from the tattered fedora that he often wore, which he adjusted at this moment to keep the sun from his eyes on a pleasant Sunday morning, Eric's style of dress was modern for the most part, simple, and mostly black. Cool. As he strolled, Eric tossed his broken pocket watch in the air, over and over, as if it were a quarter. A few women glanced back at him as he passed them on the street, but Eric's mind was once again mostly singular. He wanted a shop to repair his pocket watch, and he also wanted a good cup of coffee. Nothing fancy. He took his coffee black, no cream, no sugar. He liked the taste of coffee in its purest form. Dark, hot, like a liquid night sky sans stars. He liked the way it sloshed in his cup like the ocean at night. Many years before, he had been on a friend's boat in the evening. Eric had stepped far enough away from the edge to see the black sky mix with the dark water, seamless; there had been no beginning or end. It was all one. Some might say it had looked like a void. Nothing. But it was something, this darkness. Perhaps it was invisible to the naked eye, but the sky was still there, as were the rippling waters, stars, cool breezes, a storm.

Eric didn't have to see it to know it.

But on this sunny morning, there was no inkling of the previous evening's downpour. Even in the cooling fall weather, tourists still roamed the main city street. Eric bought a newspaper, tucked it under his arm. He observed the historic bath houses, fountains, and the gangster museum. The town of Hot Springs, aptly named for its famous mineral water that bubbles up and into public parks, lakes, and even hotel lobbies, was once a hot bed for gangsters, spiritualists, and health enthusiasts who sat in the purifying water at public bath houses. Even the great magician Houdini and his wife Bess visited the town, but Eric did not know this yet. Had he known this tidbit, he would have seen it like a bread crumb along a trail, letting Eric know he was on the right path.

Clearly lost in his own fantasies as he often was, Eric absentmindedly crossed the street and glanced at the old Grace Theatre. A teenage boy in 3-D glasses was atop the marquee, changing something about the sign. Eric paused briefly at the MJ Music Box; its marquee advertised Eddie Field and the Live Jive. At Merrick's Wax Museum, he gazed at an effigy of silent film star Glenda Goodall. Eric was about to go inside when an orange leaf tumbled over his polished shoes as the wind picked up, beckoning him to play a game of follow the leader. Eric trailed behind the leaf; they both stopped for a moment, and he looked across the street at Boots & Burdini Book Shoppe. There was a photo of him that he did not like much in the window advertising his book signing. It showed him at a table, pen in hand, with his head reclining in his other hand, staring off as if in deep thought. In reality, when he had taken the picture, there were three bright lights surrounding him, a fake backdrop, and a makeup girl that kept lathering his lips with Vaseline to make them look "more natural." There had been a fan blowing in his face to make his hair appear slightly windswept. Eric had asked, "Why would my hair be windblown indoors?" His editor at Currer, Ellis, and Acton had answered in the most honest way she knew, because to her this made perfect sense, "So women will know you're alluring." The man who wrote sexy poetry should be sexy too. The photo ended up in a celebrity magazine under the caption "America's Most Handsome Men," but the picture certainly did not capture the real Eric, or the man he was when genuinely lost in thought, writing his poems, the man he was inside. It didn't capture anything about him at all, other than the fact that it was his real fountain pen in his hand. All people saw when they looked at him were heart-shaped lips, perfectly-formed nose, and that one lock of hair that always seemed to fall sexily and haphazardly into his face. He became the poster boy for handsome writers. But it shouldn't have surprised him. Since the day his eyes turned from brown to black, he had little girls follow him home from school, leave him flowers on the doorstep, or slip love notes into his locker when he was a teenager. Eric was a walking Love Potion No. 9, his scent lingering near every woman he passed, inadvertently causing stares, sighs, and suggestions. He was not oblivious to this reaction. Not in the slightest. Being considered handsome did not bother him anymore than it would anyone else, but Eric was not vain and did not think too much about it. He certainly did not look in the mirror and see the face that everyone else was ogling, even from an early age. To him, it was just a face like any other face. Some might like it, some might not. It didn't matter ... unless it was being judged by a girl he liked, but even then, he wondered. When a little girl named Lisa had caught his eye one spring day as a boy, he had asked his grandmother what Grandpa Pilot had done to woo her.

"Needles," she had replied. "He gave me a stack of needles in a red pin cushion."

Not understanding that the gift was because Grandma Pilot loved to sew, Eric had left a set of needles stuck in a pin cushion, arranged like a face with spiky hair, on the school desk of his tiny beloved. Thinking it a giant spider, the girl had screamed and slung it across the classroom. His first attempt at romance had failed miserably, and Eric had detention for a week, missing recess, but it had given Eric something much more powerful than sweet nothings and a mutual declaration of love. It had fertilized his yearning, and he attempted his first love poem. He was starting to understand why his eyes had turned so black, black like charcoal. The poem ran two pages and was filled with sappy sentiments and one strange line that his grandmother commented on later.

"Eri," she had said, holding the little piece of paper, "what did you mean by this line: *Tiny beloved, the needles are in my heart now, but I can tell, you are not my Rosabelle.*"

He had shrugged. "I don't know. It rhymed." But he did know.

He continued from then on to write his love poetry. He gave them to no one.

By the time he was a teenager, Eric had perfected his wooing skills considerably, spending most of his days, dreamily, at the locker of a girl with springy brown hair named Angela (like an angel, he had thought). She had kept her up-turned 'do in place with a large needle, Asian style. Eric had liked to pull it out, watch her hair fall to her shoulders. Almost every morning, he would unravel her hair, but she never showed her anger, never told him that it had taken an hour to fix her hair that way. She was dating Eric Pilot, the cutest, smartest boy in school. Best to leave those things unsaid. It didn't even matter that sometimes he referenced things she did not understand. She pretended because Eric was every girl's dream, and at that time in his life, this girl was Eric's every fantasy dream sweepy romantic vision thought come to life. He might give his poems to her. It was her red lips and blue eyes that he had liked most of all. He thought her eyes and lips matched the blue & red of her cheerleading outfit. "The colors of Play-doh," he had liked to joke, but she never much got his jokes either. It didn't matter to him or to her, because for that moment, she was his world, because when Eric loved, he loved like death. It stood there, certain it would come, unmatched, undefeated, heart-wrenching and blissful at the same time. Painful and ecstatic all at once.

While every girl dreamed of him, Eric never thought about being with the prettiest girl, or the most popular. He was just looking for *his* girl. The one girl. The only girl. The singular thought in his mind. The one he had written the poems for, the one as certain as death, the one he believed in with the same knowing that the sun would rise in the morning. A love so powerful, if needed, could send a message after death. Once, well after Angela had left his teenage thoughts, he had thought he found her. Her name was Rosabelle. Her black hair had resembled the silk of a Geisha's kimono and her skin the color of a pearl. As he had sat outside the Cambridge English department, a petite girl approached him, such curves on a small frame, selling pens to raise funds for a theater class trip. She was wearing a shirt with two peaches stitched unwittingly over each breast. Now, in his mind, he found this to be the funniest thing, the way those two peaches sat perfectly over each breast – she didn't even realize it – but that soft, British voice like a young girl had such an impact, resonated so deeply in his rapidly beating heart, that he bought her entire box of pens. After all, a girl named Rosabelle had to be the girl of his dreams. His beloved. Such coincidences were not meaningless. That's what his late Grandma Pilot would have said. But had Grandma Pilot had the chance to have met Rosabelle, she would have seen past those hazel eyes into a dark heart who sold more than pens. With many coos and soft caresses, the girl quickly coerced Eric into emptying his bank account. When she was done, all he had left was a deteriorating ranch in Alaska and a scholarship, the rest of which he wouldn't receive until the following spring. He took up a job in a bookstore; she took off to California to be a movie star, which she is to this day, although you may know her by a very different name.

For awhile his eyes lightened, heart slowed. Back then, his love life was like bathing in lukewarm water; it never felt hot enough, never completely right. His affection was genuine, although tears never rolled out of his eyes when he made love to them. Eventually his eyes darkened, his heart went back in step with his soul, but none of this via any woman, mind you. It was from the deep yearning he first felt as a boy. That yearning, the longing within him so strong. So he wrote his books and he waited. His thoughts eventually becoming so singular it was like looking through a fisheye lens, the thing in focus standing out in the center – his beloved.

Now, on this lazy Sunday morning in Hot Springs, as a bee buzzed near his ear, the leaf Eric had been following finally stopped, landing at the doorstep of the Rosabelle Café. Eric dropped his pocket watch, shattering the glass on the sidewalk. Eric's black eyes only focused on the word "Rosabelle."

A yellow canary sat on the windowsill. It cocked its head side to side, watching Dawn make breakfast. Bacon for herself, a piece of toast for the quiet little bird. Dawn pushed open the window with some struggle; the paint had hardened around the sill and kept it in place. The bird did not fly away, only hopped back a few steps waiting, knowing Dawn had something to give. She crumbled the piece of bread and left it on the windowsill. She watched the bird eat, quickly pecking and bobbing its small head. He had to be someone's pet, and they had set him free ... or he had escaped. Somewhere in the yard, she heard the drumming of bees. Dawn looked up to the blue sky. A biplane circled.

Sunday was always Dawn's favorite day of the week. On that day, things had always been quiet at the vineyard. Her mother spent that day alone in her office going over the accounting books. Dawn could roam the house in peace. But that wasn't the only reason Dawn liked that day. It was the beginning of a new week, the hope that things would change.

While she stared out at that blue sky, dressed for spring not fall, and ready to walk out into that sunny day, Eric entered the Rosabelle Café. He did not look around. He walked in as if he had been there before, as if he knew the place, the way someone walks into their own home, aware, knowing where everything is. Much different than the way Dawn would walk in much later, surveying everything timidly.

No one would mistake Dawn for an adventurer, but she had an orderly way of doing things; it was important for her to learn every step, every block, every stoplight on each corner. She had to make a mental map of her new town – the grocery store on this block, flea markets on this street, museum at this end – and see what was safe and what was not.

After breakfast, she grabbed her purse and left the apartment, ready to survey her new surroundings. A bird chirped at her; she swore it was the same canary. She walked into the garden to look for it, and Mitch ran over to her, playfully snapping at her ankles. He put his paws up on her legs and accidentally pulled a loose thread from her hem. Dawn unraveled it and tossed it on the ground. Mrs. Crumper, working in her garden, reached down and plucked a wilted petal from a vine. "Perhaps it's been a bit too much rain. All this rain has drowned out some of my mums," she said referring to her plants when she saw Dawn. "At least my licorice is okay. You ever had licorice root tea?"

"I didn't know you could make tea from it."

"Oh, sure. Just like any herbal tea. It's good for my arthritis. I'll make you some when I get these harvested and dried." Mrs. Crumper put her glasses on – she kept them on a chain around her neck – and inspected Leon the Gnome. "Mitch, for the blasted last time, stop peeing on me Leon!" she yelled at the dog after having noticed a sticky yellow trail on the gnome's vest. With a stick in his mouth, and as if he understood and did not care, Mitch wagged his tail at Dawn's feet. She took the stick and threw it. Off he went towards a rundown corner of the yard; Mitch sniffed around a set of abandoned beekeeper's hives. Some lonely bees still buzzed.

"Odd they are still out this late in the year," said Mrs. Crumper, noticing Dawn interest in the bees. "My husband, rest his lovely soul, was a beekeeper."

"I'm allergic to bees," Dawn said but she was not. Many times as a child she had been stung and never flinched. If she could catch one, she always would, and wonder why it stung her because now it would die. The protection of honey was that important?

"Is it serious?" Mrs. Crumper asked.

"Oh, no," Dawn continued to lie. "I just swell up a little."

"The bees still live there, rent free. I don't tend 'em. I s'pose I should get rid of 'em but they remind me too much of my Henry."

Mitch came back with the stick. Dawn took it and

threw it again. With glee, he ran after it. "I never had a dog before," Dawn said.

"Never?" Mrs. Crumper asked, bathing the gnome in a bird bath.

"My mother was allergic. We did have two cats and a canary though." All this was true.

Mrs. Crumper stopped washing the gnome and pondered. "Hopefully, not at the same time."

A memory came over Dawn and a faint smile rested on her face. Not amused, not saddened. It was a memory that resided in her thoughts like an empty boat floating calmly in a lake. Content.

"It was a little like Sylvester and Tweety," Dawn lied.

"I can imagine!"

With a voice, dry and cold like an Alaskan wind, Dawn said, "They ate him."

Mrs. Crumper nearly dropped the gnome. "Glory be!"

In a perversely macabre voice, Dawn explained the scenario as if telling a spooky story. "I came home from school one day. The cage knocked to the floor, open. Feathers everywhere. Blood on the floor."

Hugging the wet gnome to her breasts, Mrs. Crumper listened intently like a child hearing a story about a hook-handed killer in the woods during a camp fire. "You poor dear. You must have been horrified."

"Not really. It was my mother's bird." But that wasn't how it had happened at all. The bird's song had always been sad; its eyes hollow and small (tiny because it had never seen the world). It had been born in a cage, lived in a cage, and would die in a cage. Dawn couldn't let that happen. She knew the key had to be in her mother's office where everything was neatly arranged and labeled. Dawn had simply opened a large filing cabinet, located a folder marked "bird cage key," and took it (remembering to replace it immediately). The fake blood, the feathers, all purchased at a flea market from a junk dealer and moonshiner of questionable age who knew damned well that Dawn stole from most of the vendors, but he didn't care. He respected her sneaky and nonchalant approach, selling her his wares for half the cost.

"Still, must have been a terrible sight for a young girl," Mrs. Crumper said, placing Leon back in his regular spot.

"Oddly enough there was a canary outside my window today," Dawn said, as a still-green leaf, resisting fall foliage, tumbled past. The leaf, topsy-turvy as if it were doing cartwheels, rolled out of the yard onto the street. It stopped, as if by magic, on the corner of Third and Rahner. A gust of window picked it up, tossed it downtown. Dawn looked up to the sky; the biplane was circling. "Have you ever seen that bird before, the yellow canary?"

"Can't say that I have," she answered.

"I'm going downtown," Dawn said. She was used to telling people about her whereabouts (sometimes lying about it). It was a habit she knew she could stop now, but she acted on rote.

Mitch, who had chased down the stick only to be distracted by something underneath an apple tree, wagged his tail as he snorted about. "Bye, Mitch," Dawn said, walking over and patting him on the head. Talking to dogs was also easy; they almost always smiled back.

"Mitch, get away from the apples," Mrs. Crumper said, shooing him away. "I'm a bit superstitious about it."

"Why?" Dawn asked. "Dogs and apple trees?"

"Old wives tale. If ripe apples and blossoms are on the tree at the same time, it's an omen that someone is about to die."

"I'm not afraid of death."

Mrs. Crumper patted her on the back. "Love, I didn't mean you, or anyone really, just a silly superstition."

For all his belief in magic, Eric was not superstitious. Eric enjoyed walking under ladders and crossing the paths of black cats. He liked the way it rattled the nerves of others. Those things, he knew, had no basis in reality. Most people would say the things that Eric did believe in had no basis in reality either; however, very few could deny that Eric understood and knew things that others did not. It wasn't a sixth sense. It wasn't ESP or any psychic ability, because most of those things, he believed, could be explained away. Intuition maybe. But it seemed outside of the realm of psychology or science or any conventional sense of spirituality. It was like being a telephone wire. Each ring for him reverberated, flowed over him, into him, and he knew someone was calling. At that moment, ordering a cup of coffee in the Rosabelle Café, he waited for the next ring.

Dawn, on the other hand, journeyed on and never saw the obvious. For someone so suspicious, someone so cautious that she needed to make a mental map of her surroundings, she never noticed the things right in her face. If she had, strolling downtown, she would have seen the "America's Most Handsome" poster in the bookstore window across the street. Instead, Dawn ignored it all, traveled straight on through, but like that lonely bee who had found a flower atop a hotel, Dawn was about to stumble upon a one-in-a-million chance. Because, you see, fate never misses a beat. Through the window of the Rosabelle Café, Dawn saw Eric inside, reading a newspaper, sipping a cup of coffee.

A wavy loose thread of hair covering one eye, his hat pulled a little low, Eric tilted his head upward as if he felt her presence. The lid holding everything together in her mind blew straight off. Through the window, he looked her in the eye ... locked those pitch black eyes of his with something flickering within right on her. Red-gold-then-orange. Dawn quickly looked away, but not quick enough to miss his warm smile, but fast enough to miss his wave to come inside to join him. A gust of wind blew a series of green and orange leaves in the air, blocking her view for a moment of what was up ahead. Dawn ignored him, pretended Eric was not inside, and walked on. She did, however, remember the name of the café.

As morning receded, the shadows cast along the sidewalk signaled afternoon, and Eric stared out the window as if a silhouette lingered, as if Dawn's thoughts remained too (and they did). That girl, although she had walked on – and he noted that she had done it quickly – she had seen him. Eric stared at nothing in particular outside, sipping his coffee, content and happy. He would see her again. All this focus on nothing outside annoyed the café girl behind the counter, who had been watching him all morning, hoping to get his attention. She eyed him as if he were the most delicious chocolate cake she had ever seen. Eric's concentration was only disrupted by a ding-ding noise – the bell above the door. In walked the teenage boy he had seen earlier outside the marquee of the theater in 3-D glasses. He had since stashed the glasses, had a satchel in his hand, and was now staring vaguely at the menu. Up close, he looked like Jughead from the *Archie* comics. Absentmindedly, Eric held up his newspaper and scanned it. The teenage boy, who had stopped staring at the menu and was now watching Eric, noticed the photo on the back of Eric's newspaper. "That's you!" the boy said.

Eric turned the paper over, looked at the ad. He had an interview with this same paper on Tuesday. "Yes, it is," Eric replied and nonchalantly went back to reading the front page.

"Crazy!" the boy said, trying to sound hip, but his nerdy appearance and uncombed hair suggested otherwise.

A few others in the café stopped sipping their lattes or mochas or frappichiniweeniwhateverohs and looked at Eric too. The café girl put her breasts up on the countertop (venti size), stroked her blond hair, and licked her lips. When Eric had come inside earlier, she had dropped an entire box of straws. Trying to hide the flicker in his eyes was like trying to hide a willow tree in a desert. Eric's passionate side stood out like an oasis. The café girl was even more excited that he was in the newspaper. She adjusted her ventis.

Sensing the invading eyes, Eric put the newspaper away and tinkered with his broken watch. Through the window, the sunlight reflected off the broken glass of the watch like a kaleidoscope. Reflected in the broken glass was a biplane circling high above outside. He imagined the whir-whir of the engine, the happy pilot sailing next to the white clouds, and each smiling person who looked upwards to admire the plane.

"Tragic," the teenage boy said, seeing Eric's broken watch.

"It's not just the glass. It seems to be stuck too," Eric replied, fingering the watch hands.

The boy introduced himself as Travis Edwards, pretending to be cool ala *Shaft* or a 1960s Vegas lounge lizard. "Ticker no flicker? No tick no tock? No trouble. I can fix it. I build robots. It's just a little mechanical razzle dazzle."

"I'm sure you can, but this is an antique watch. Do you know a repair shop?"

Travis shrugged. "I can probably find one. I haven't lived here long, but I know my way around."

"There's one on Third," the girl behind the counter said.

Travis, seemingly a little disappointed, took a seat on a sofa on the other side of the café and counted change from his pocket, glancing at the prices of the drinks on the menu. Eric took another sip of coffee but got the hint, amused.

"Travis, if you go down to that shop and ask about my watch, I'll give you ... " Eric held up his hands, fluttered his fingers, and pulled a ten dollar bill from his palm. "Ten bucks."

"Hot tamales and get your lemons!" Travis exclaimed with a leg slap, mimicking the catch phrase of B-movie director Glen "Jonesy" Jones. "How'd you do that?"

"Magic."

The café girl, still in hopes of catching Eric's attention, said, "You should visit the Grace Theatre. They're bringing back the magic shows starting this coming weekend."

Travis nodded in agreement and said, "I work there sometimes."

She ignored Travis, still in hopes. "I could show you," she said to Eric, coquettish.

"I saw that place on the way over," Eric said. "I know my way." Disappointed, the girl gave up and went about cleaning the counter (keeping her ventis off display). Eric pulled out a deck of cards from his back pocket, shuffled them, and rolled the stack up and down his arm. After shuffling them every conceivable way – Travis never taking his eyes off Eric – he asked Travis to pick a card, any card. The boy did so, memorized it, and stuck it back in the deck. After reshuffling, Eric said like a mystic, "Your card is in the sports section of the paper." Travis picked up the newspaper, found the section and his card – nine of hearts.

With a grin, Travis said, "Watch this. It's a real ring-a-ding trick." He reached into his bag, took out three red balls, and juggled them.

"That's pretty good," Eric replied just as Travis dropped all three red balls. They scattered over the café, and he did not scurry to catch them. Eric merely grinned and reached for his newspaper again. "Tell the watch shop that I have a 1926 Waltham railroad pocket watch, open face, with a winding key."

"Will do," Travis said, walking over to Eric's table and pulling out a handful of keys. They were all looped together like a set you might see hanging from the belt of a building superintendent, the key to every room.

"Gotta have the right key," Travis said.

"You old enough to drive?" Eric asked.

"Padlock. For my bike." He nodded to the bicycle outside. The bike looked like it was pieced together from various parts, one of which could have been part of a fender from an old car. Travis found his key, gathered the red balls that were hiding about the café (under a chair, a table, and one customer's crossed legs), and went to find the watch repair shop.

In the sky, the biplane still circled. Eric looked down at his watch, then looked at the clock on the wall. They both said 1:26 p.m.

It was almost time ...

A few blocks up, with two large stone gargoyles on either side of her, Dawn had been sitting on the steps of the museum for a long time, contemplating. The chances of running into the same person twice are quite slim. She could walk back to the Rosabelle Café and order a hot chocolate. Maybe Earl Gray? No, hot chocolate seemed right – something sweeter. He would still be there. She could see the café from the museum. The only person who had come out was a teenage boy who had set off on his bike in the opposite direction as if he were on a special mission, his legs pumping up and down on the bike rapidly. A biplane kept circling the sky, casting shadows when it flew over head. A bee landed on her knee, did not sting her, and flew back toward the café. The wind was starting to pick up and she felt cold. Dawn took a deep breath, stood up, looked back at the museum door (closed on Sunday), and walked down the steps.

In the end, she could not bring herself to do it. It did not matter at that moment though, because two people who are meant to be together are akin to bees making honey. It is the nature of the thing and can't be changed. Lovers meeting is an in-born process that must and will occur, no matter the circumstances, no matter the consequences. There will be honey. Even in autumn.

With leaves changing color all around her, Dawn walked back home on the opposite side of the street (failing to see America's Most Handsome again). One quick glance across the street, and yes, he was still inside the café – his hat down, his eyes tinkering with something that glinted like shiny metal. With sunlight on her face, Dawn headed toward Rahner Street and Eric smiled.

Sunshine

It is imperative that valuable items be protected from exposure to sunlight, moisture, and dirt. The museum handbook lay open on Dawn's desk, but she did not read over these words. She knew the drill. Always the same. Routine rules. The workroom was dark with the exception of work lights treated with UV light filters. Heavy curtains covered the windows. It was impossible to tell the time of day, if it were raining, if it were sunny. The only stream of light that defied the odds seeped in from the outer hallway that led to the public museum, which housed everything from the first winning ticket from the Oaklawn Race Track to a saxophone once belonging to President Clinton.

Dawn adjusted the lamp on her desk. Straightened, organized, aligned. She looked over the contents on the table. Magnifying glass. Check. Rubber cement eraser. Check. X-Acto knife. Deacidification spray. Check check. She sorted various folders and sleeves, then moved a pen that tested pH levels until it rested exactly perpendicular to a tub of putty-like cleaner used to wipe away mold and stains.

From the corner, the janitor, who dressed like one of

the Temptations, shiny silver suit and patent leather shoes, watched her as he methodically mopped the floor working his way backwards out the door. Dawn appreciated that, cleaning in an organized manner, but she did not enjoy him staring at her. She put on one white cotton glove and walked over to a large wooden filing cabinet that had over-sized flat drawers. With un-gloved hand, she opened a drawer marked "Houdini" and removed a series of large folders with her gloved hand. As she took these back to her desk, the janitor said, "Michael Jackson was the last of the great showmen." He nodded at the white glove, his voice as silky as Motown, and added, "One glove. Michael Jackson."

"I wear two," she said, pointing at the other glove on her desk. "It keeps dirt and oil off the documents."

A slow nod. He moonwalked out the door holding the mop handle like a microphone. The rest of the employees ignored him, just as they ignored Dawn. When they had to speak to her, they did, but mostly Dawn was like furniture, an object to be interacted with when necessary. Dawn lived on the outskirts of conversation, overhearing each word, never adding her voice to the mix.

A little voice in her head was trying to remember where she had heard the name Rosabelle before. Was it at the train station? It was like trying to remember the last name of a character on an old television show, stuck in your mind, on the tip of your tongue. When it finally comes, it's like an epiphany, a mental head-thump. Although she received no such revelation, seeing Eric three mornings in a row at the Rosabelle had felt like some sort of sign. Three times in three days. What were the chances? Even Dawn could not put logic to that. They say third time is the charm, and Dawn had wanted to tempt fate this Tuesday morning, but she was too shy to go inside the café. He was always in the same spot as if waiting for her (which he was). This morning had been the same. Clutching the handle of her lunch box in both hands, she had paused long enough for him to notice, but he had already seen her coming. He always saw her coming. Beyond Dawn's perky attire, beyond her shyness, he could see her. Even with both of his hands wrapped around his coffee cup, Dawn could tell he was smiling. A small nod and he had let her walk on again. To open the door for Dawn would be like putting a baby's hand on a cup of hot coffee. The heat would cause a burn. She would come to him and he would wait, in the place he was suppose to, the Rosabelle Café, because he knew from her curiosity, that she was ready for a drink.

It was close to noon and Dawn already felt parched. There was a fan blowing in the workroom but it still felt stuffy. As if on cue, an arctic breeze swept through the room. Absolute zero. No life stirring. It was as if every employee had been zapped with a ray-gun that froze them like snowmen. The frozen sea that suddenly flowed into the room was Mrs. Lawley, the head of the historical society patrons. She wore a linen suit the color of dog excrement. Her bunned hair sat curled like a pile of cat poop, and her breath reminded Dawn of Leon the Gnome's pee-ridden body. She had her mother's harsh blue eyes. Everyone in the room stayed motionless as if the slightest movement might illicit some sort of reaction from Mrs. Lawley, but acting nonchalant was an art form Dawn had perfected. So often in her life, she did not get what she wanted and had to pretend not to care.

"Aren't you little Miss Sunshine," Mrs. Lawley said derogatory.

That morning Dawn's eyes had lingered long enough at the Rosabelle Café to notice a poster advertising "Mrs. Sunshine's Crumb Cakes Sold Exclusively Inside." Eric had a slice in front of him, a little crumb on his shirt (she had lingered long enough to notice that too). This memory made Dawn smile inside, not outside so everyone else could see, but it kept her warm as Mrs. Lawley inspected Dawn as if searching her for tiny crumbs. She got close, almost close enough to be somewhat creepy, and examined Dawn as if she were a piece of yellowed parchment on display in the museum. Was she an antique? A genuine artifact? Any flaws? Did she belong there?

"Houdini?" Mrs. Lawley asked. Dictator. Demanding an answer to something that was not a question. "Still dead, I take it?"

With Mrs. Lawley's mean beady eyes on her, the room was still frozen, but thinking about Eric cracked the tundra, giving Dawn a peek of blue ocean beneath ice. Dawn looked at her, right in the eyes, and said, "There's a stain on the poster. I'm cleaning it off."

Mrs. Lawley seemed satisfied with that response, if such a thing were possible for such a woman, and walked away to annoy and interrogate the other employees.

Dawn rubbed her neck, stretched, and went to the breakroom. After buying a cherry Coke, she took her lunch box – yellow sun painted on the front – from the refrigerator. She sat down and put it in her lap, hiding it, hiding her thoughts. See, she had told herself that morning, after seeing Eric for the third time, that she would make herself go back at lunch. Be brave and see. Just see. Maybe he had lunch there too? Seeing Eric once again ... would the fourth time be as equally bewitching?

These thoughts ran through her mind, bouncing around like a pinball. Everything and everyone around her was a bit vague, but she was aware of most of it. There was an advertisement for a Day of the Dead festival tacked to the bulletin board. Someone had etched "10 Wms" into the table. Near her, a man was reading a newspaper called *The Radem Times* (a small town somewhere between Texas and Louisiana). He flipped the paper over, said to no one in particular, "Sophie Bess has a new movie." Sophie, "America's sweetheart," was the box office rival of Eric's one-time money-stealing beloved, although Dawn would never know this. As a matter of fact, no one would ever know that Sophie's rival was the once lover of the then-unknown poet. Because even the former Rosabelle, knew her deception ran deep.

Lost in some daydream, the man muttered, still admiring Sophie, "So pretty." Dawn found it never mattered to learn anyone's name. Most people were like characters in a bad movie. She watched them, felt bored, and went about her day. And like those characters, they would never turn and look at her, the girl watching from the crowd. People noticed her like the sky, not part of the action, not part of the story.

"Keep dreaming," said another employee. "Sophie's already found her one true love."

Coming up behind her, the janitor startled Dawn with a gentle tap to her shoulder with his broom. In his silky soul voice, he sang the words, "Who's loving you?"

"What?" she said, barely audible.

The conversation around her continued. "You need to keep up with gossip," the man reading the paper said. "She's on the outs with her husband."

"Is that so?"

"Really?"

"Didn't read that."

Back and forth it went.

At the sink, a heavy-set female employee, who had her back turned to everyone, washed out a skull-and-crossbones coffee mug and said, "They're still together." Very matter-of-fact, as if she knew the actress and her husband. She took a seat by Dawn, ignored her, and joined in the conversation. The janitor, still behind Dawn, kept trying to get her attention. Dawn ignored him. The woman beside her rambled on about gossip magazines. Her hair was held in place with a stick that infomercials advertised as "versatile" for many hairdos. It was currently keeping her hair in some sort of V-formation on the back of her head. Announcing it like Mary Hart, the woman said, "But sources say she *is* having an affair with a pilot."

Something about the word "pilot" resonated with Dawn like the name Rosabelle. The janitor tapped her again, sang the phrase "Who's loving you?" in a very beautiful voice. He caressed the broom like a microphone and proceeded to sing *Who's Loving You* as eloquently as the Jackson Five's lead singer. Everyone paused. He flopped a flyer on the table advertising Eddie Field and the Live Jive playing "one night only" at the MJ Music Box with a photo of the janitor next to the words "with special guest Sledge."

"You sing?" one employee asked because it had never occurred to anyone that a janitor, an uneducated man who mopped floors and cleaned toilets and wiped away their gunk from the microwave could possibly have a talent or a passion or do anything of any sort worthwhile in comparison to their important museum job.

"Of course he sings!" said a loud voice at the door. Dawn turned to see a young man with curly hair and wire-rimmed glasses wearing a dragon T-shirt that Mrs. Crumper would have loved. He patted Sledge and said, "See you at the MJ Saturday night," and flopped down across from Dawn. "You're new," he said, taking her by surprise. She nodded, told him her name. "I'm Will Week. Everyone calls me Mr. Google, because I can find anything anywhere anytime. I've just returned from the bowels of hell, but it's nice to meet you." They shook hands and he walked over to the vending machine.

"Did you find anything?" one employee asked Will.

"Naturally. Yeah, the estate sale was incredible. My Capone work will be a masterpiece. We are talking AP stories people. A freakin' P." Will had a Ph.D from Stanford in archeology, but gave up field work on ancient cultures when he discovered his love of early twentieth century gangsters. He took several trips a year to Chicago and had just returned from an auction and estate sale of one of the relatives of Al Capone's former cohorts. He planned to compile all of his research into a book to be sold exclusively through the museum. Unlike Houdini's brief visit to the city, Hot Springs was a widely known vacation spot for Capone.

Will searched around in his pocket for change, watched Dawn take petite sips of soda, and asked, "You're working on Houdini?"

She looked up, realizing he was talking to her. "Yes. Houdini."

"Awesome. I wanted those papers, I'll admit, but c'est la vie. It wasn't meant to be for me, but for you." Will dropped three quarters, clink clink clink, into the vending machine. A package of marshmallows gently hit the slot.

Dawn sat up a little straighter, remembering.

"This machine is broken," Will said. "I didn't hit D3." He held the bag up, asking if anyone wanted marshmallows. The grandfather clock in the museum hall struck noon and sounded throughout the building. Dawn motioned that she wanted the marshmallows. She took her lunch box, and a deep breath, and walked outside.

Still in the café, Eric had already refreshed his coffee three times. His stomach grumbled; the slice of crumb cake had not been enough, but that little ripple in his gut told him to wait just a little while more. His journal was on the table, and he jotted down bits, pieces, and observations. Before long, he heard the ding-ding of the bell above the door, saw a little drop of rain hit the window. He smelled her perfume, pure sugar, before he looked up at Dawn, that girl who had the sensibility of a lemur or meerkat, always on alert about predators.

Clutching her lunch box, Dawn shifted from foot to foot, nervous-like but with head held high in confidence (but she felt no such certainty). She had learned such bravado from her mother. She looked about the room cautiously, deliberately ignoring Eric, observing, and placed an order.

Eric liked the way her Southern accent said "strawberry" with a drawn out "straw" and a little lilt in "berry" when she ordered her smoothie. He kept writing in his notebook, but he was only doodling now, paying attention to her words instead, stealing quick glances. All she wanted to do was stare at him too. It's funny about people – what we most want, we pretend to ignore. Dawn loved the way his pen sounded on the paper, kind of scratchy but smooth. With drink in hand, she glanced back at him. He put his pen down.

"Looks like we both made it to our destination," Eric said, standing. Dawn's feet were mired to the floor. Politely she smiled, holding that drink in front of her like a locked gate. Eric motioned for her to sit down, pulled the chair out for her. Open. One step and two. Fate winning out as always, and there they sat, facing one another, as they had done on the train.

He left his notebook open, only scooting it over to the side, next to the fountain pen. Dawn put her lunch box and drink on the table and held out her hand, formal, and said, "Dawn. Dawn Corner." Shaking her hand, imitating the formality, he responded, "Eric. Eric Pilot." The warmth of his hand stunned her. She held it for a second too long, looked into his eyes for a moment too much. Red-gold-then-orange. One touch, the warm look in his black eyes, but the flicker was within her too and Eric saw it.

"Settled into your new place?" he asked.

She nodded. "Mostly. I'm waiting on some furniture. You?"

"Oh," Eric replied, a bit uneasy, "I'm not staying. I'm only here a short time." Dawn tried to hide her disappointment, but Eric saw that too. The little ember that had started to re-ignite had just been doused with a drop of rain. He saw the rain falling outside, harder now, but just a shower. Dawn watched it too.

"Rain follows me, I think," she said.

He smiled compassionately. "Little dark cloud over your head?"

"I think so." She tried to say it casual, but it came out sad.

Eric added, referring to the town, "This is my last stop. I like it here though. It's nice."

She pointed to his notebook, and with a response that was far too quick, far too nonchalant, she asked, "What are you writing?"

"A little of this, a little of that." Eric tapped his notebook.

She opened her lunch box. Inside, she had stuffed the bag of marshmallows that Will had given her. She took out each item, turkey sandwich, Fritos, and Mr. Goodyum, carefully. Eric watched just as carefully. One haphazard movement and she would run.

She tried not to stammer when she said, "I brought you –" Almost.

Eric raised an eyebrow. Waiting ...

"Do you want marshmallows?" Finally. Hoping. The weird moment of fear and quiet.

"The little clouds," Eric said, taking the package. "Thank you." He opened them and poured a few into her lunch box. "White fluffy clouds. Not rain clouds. They'll chase the rain away."

"I don't think that'll work," she said.

"You never know." His smile, something, she could not place. Genuine? For her?

"How long are you staying?" Still hope, although she did not want to admit it.

Eric's response was slow. He wanted to push away that dark cloud forever. "I have a commitment on Saturday, but I'm going to stay a few more days. Beautiful here." Red-gold-then-orange. "I'm leaving next Tuesday, Halloween." He ate a marshmallow slowly then picked up his fountain pen, twirling it between his fingers ... waiting.

Whenever Dawn felt attracted to a man, she quickly made a list of his good qualities in her mind, then she listed every conceivable way he could hurt her, then the list of ways he would eventually leave her life. Before she could finish her list of Eric's qualities – dark eyes, nice hair, mysterious – she found the top and only item on the list of ways he would leave – he was only in Hot Springs for a short time.

"Well," she said, disappointed and returning to her businesslike demeanor, "You said on the train that you're from Alaska. I've never been to Alaska. I don't travel much. I'm sure it's lovely." His hands are nice too, she thought to herself, and the way he plays with the gold fountain pen, a real fountain pen, then added that to her list of good qualities. The longer she stayed, the longer the list would get.

"Do you work at that museum a few blocks up? History museum right?"

She nodded, nearly blushed. He had remembered that.

"You like it?" he asked, putting his pen down and eating another marshmallow, this time popping it into his mouth quickly, hungry.

"It's interesting."

"What kind of things do you catalog?"

She shrugged. "Right now I'm working on a collection of Houdini memorabilia."

The fountain pen rolled off the table on its own. Eric left it there. This time it was his voice that was nearly a whisper, a little wisp of sound like a swirl of smoke. "I love Houdini."

"You were reading a book about him on the train." Her voice was soft in remembrance.

She had remembered that, he thought. Eric was without words. His notebook sat open but he could think of no words to put there, no word big enough. His pen out of reach. He didn't move, made no indication of what he was thinking. His pupils dilated – the flash of something red-gold-then-orange was a warm fireplace in winter. Was it too warm? No. Intense yes, so Dawn glanced down to pick up his pen. The gold pen solitary on the floor, gleaming in the sunlight that streamed in through the window. The rain had stopped. She shivered and handed him the pen, their fingers touching briefly.

"A lot of people don't know Houdini did a show here," Dawn said.

"I didn't. No." Eric looked around him. It all seemed surreal for a moment, sitting in a café named Rosabelle, talking about Houdini with a beautiful girl. The thoughts in his head spun like a top. He stood up, pulled his wallet from his back pocket, feeling a little awkward. "I'm going to get something to eat. You want anything else?"

Dawn shook her head, wondering why he was suddenly uncomfortable. What had she done? Said? With a snide glare from the café girl, Dawn felt like a teenager walking past Luanne Mixen. This time, however, there was something she had never seen in Luanne's mean stare – it was fear. Luanne and her group of friends had been confident in their looks; any boy they wanted – fingersnap! – and he was there. There were no doubts, no shortcomings, no fear. It was Dawn who had all of those. Mimicking the syrup-laden voice that Luanne had always used around boys, the café girl took Eric's order, hoping he would lap it up like a kitten to milk, but Dawn saw the look of fear in that woman's eyes, the depression sinking into her fake grin. Dawn knew it all too well, had seen it in her reflection many times. Eric had rejected that girl; for this, Dawn was certain. Where had this buxom, blonde-haired woman failed? What was he looking for that would give Dawn a chance?

She ate a marshmallow, tried to casually steal a peek at his journal, and waited while he placed his order for a turkey croissant sandwich and Sunkist soda. "No cheese," he said. Eric tapped his foot a few times, unlike him to be impatient, and looked back at Dawn with a grin. When he turned back around to the counter, Dawn tried to peek again at his words. She could not read them, but she saw doodles of keys, hearts, and flames. In the corner, he had drawn the sun rising. Outside sunlight was gleaming on the wet pavement, streaming across their table and onto the floor – the same spot he had dropped his fountain pen. She looked at the pen; it was engraved with "From Ehrich."

Eric came back to the table with his food, and Dawn asked, as he peeked between the croissant halves, "You don't like cheese?"

He shook his head. "I don't eat dairy."

"Lactose intolerant?"

"Moo intolerant."

"What?"

"It's the sound of the moo that gets me."

"That doesn't ... "

"The moo. Freaks me out."

"You're afraid of cows?"

"Not cows. The moo. Ever since I saw my grand-father grab that teat and milk that cow and mooooo ... well, I haven't had dairy since."

She added funny to her list, remembering again his joke about the Coca-Cola polar bears in Alaska. This time, she did not try to stifle her laugh. She let it out. The café girl glared at her again, a full-on pout, but Dawn did not see.

"Sun's shining," he said, taking a bite, but he was not referring to the weather. She nodded.

"Did you see that place in the train station? Mademoiselle Danielle's Parisian Ice Cream? How can French ice cream be any different?"

"I wouldn't know being that I have an aversion to moos, but I once read an article about the owner, who is from Georgia, and she claims it's made with French cows. I grew up around cows and I happen to know there is no such thing. She wants us to assume the cows wear little berets and sit outside cafes near the Eiffel Tower."

Dawn laughed again. "You grew up on a farm then?"

"We had a ranch. Some horses, cows. My grand-parents were vets, specialized in livestock, farm animals. I grew up around a lot of animals."

"Did you live with your grandparents?"

"Since I was seven. My parents were killed in a car crash." He still spelled out "collision" in his head but did not like to say it. "This little car. It was so small – " Eric pinched his fingers together to indicate the size. " – and yet it crushed my parents' big car. Little could crush big. I learned that."

Dawn's feelings about death were the polar opposite of Eric's, because she had never felt love, but somewhere inside her the flame had been lit, and Dawn took one of the marshmallows he had put in her lunch box and put it on his plate. "Sometimes little can crush big in a good way."

"Chase the rain clouds away," he said and ate the marshmallow. "Thank you."

"I grew up on a grape farm."

"Grape farm?" he asked, popping open his soda.

"Vineyard actually. In Altus. My family made wine."

"Cool." He took a long drink.

She shrugged. "Not really."

"At least grapes don't make any noise like cows."

"They probably want to."

"Why do you say that?"

"They start off green and grow in the rain and sunlight, and when they get plump and purple, their stems are ripped off. They get crushed by cold steel and left to sour in a sealed vat."

"That's quite ... an interesting way of looking at it."

"I still like wine though ... and I like dairy."

"You ain't afraid of no moo," he said, parodying the line from the *Ghostbusters* theme song.

"You're silly," she said, girlishly and felt embarrassed.

Eric always knew the right thing to say at the right moment, and he sensed her embarrassment, but his reasons for changing the subject were for himself this time. "What are you archiving on Houdini exactly?" He took a big bite of his sandwich. This time it was he who played nonchalant. A little flake of croissant stuck to the corner of his mouth. He did not feel it there; Dawn felt embarrassed again, because she wanted to touch his mouth, remove it for him. The little crumb dropped onto this plate. He dabbed it with his finger and ate it.

"I'm cataloging some old documents, newspaper clippings, ads from his visit here," she answered.

"Any letters?" He took a napkin from a container

that was sitting on the corner of the table and wiped his mouth. Eric was a hearty eater; Dawn a nibbler in public. She pinched at her sandwich, pulled off the bread crusts, played with the corn chips. But when she was alone ... alone was different.

"There's a letter from his wife," Dawn said, answering his question.

"Bess?" he asked softly, as if referring to the name of an old friend.

"Beatrice Houdini."

He smiled. "She liked to go by Bess though. Her name was actually Wilhemina Beatrice."

"Did you memorize the biography?" She meant it to be funny and he did smile.

"I'm a little bit of a historian myself."

"On the private lives of magicians?"

"Maybe." He winked, stretched, took another drink. He finally adjusted to the surreal moment, at least surreal to him. The world around them continued on. The sun had chased the rain away. The girl at the counter waited on customers and occasionally threw him a seductive still-hopeful glance. There were other customers eating and talking. People passed by on the sidewalk. Nothing out of the ordinary. But Eric saw so much more.

He continued his dissertation of Houdini information as if he were reading from an encyclopedia. "She went by Bess Houdini. Harry's real name was Ehrich Weiss. Spelled E-H-R-I-C-H, but pronounced like my name." He paused, as if waiting for a reaction. He got none because Dawn did not notice such things. "I always thought that was cool."

"My middle name is Beatrice."

Eric did notice such things. "Your middle name is Beatrice." It was a statement, not a question. A soft voice. Bess. But Dawn only shrugged, nodded, and said, "It was my great-grandmother's name."

He picked up his fountain pen, pointed out the inscription. "This use to belong to Sir Arthur Conan Doyle."

"Wow."

"Given to him by Ehrich Weiss."

"That's what that means on your – " She stopped herself because she did not want Eric to know that she had been looking at the pen earlier. "They were friends?"

Eric nodded. "For awhile."

"What happened?"

"They had certain disagreements, varying viewpoints you might say, on matters of a spiritual nature." He took another bite of his sandwich.

"You certainly know your Houdini facts."

"If he were alive, I'd be a stalker," he said with his mouth full.

Dawn laughed. "Why do you like Houdini so much?" She collected information like conducting an interview for a magazine, not like a girl falling in love (although she was). She did not know that Eric was essentially doing the same but in a completely different (and mystical) way.

"I like magic," Eric answered.

"I'm not a big fan of magic." Dawn said it defensively, like a guilty witness on the stand, but it was true. She did not. Her interest in Houdini was based on their shared love of escape. She liked Houdini for his ability to crack safes, wrangle out of handcuffs, and slip out of a straightjacket. At least, this is what she believed then.

"How could you not like magic?"

"It's not real."

"Card tricks. Rabbits out of hats. All illusions. This is true. But magic is real."

"That doesn't make sense, Eric." It was the first time she said his name out loud. Eric. Eric. Eric! It resonated in her ears, hummed in her mouth. It was as if it had an aroma like a fine wine and permeated up through her nose into her lungs through her heart. Eric. And, yet, she didn't believe in magic.

He noticed it too, with the little flutter of her eyes when she said Eric, especially the way she drew out his name with a heavy emphasis on the "K" sound. "Houdini spent a great deal of his life calling out hucksters and charlatans, fake spiritualists, but I think, deep down, he was always hoping to find real magic, Dawn."

Hearing him say her name was even better. Her heart was still warming like a new chick from an egg, adjusting to life, to wings, to the beat-beat-beat of a thumping heart. She wasn't quite ready to stand on two legs and walk, but her heart had imprinted on Eric and instinctively she was following him. Eric ... that name. "Did you know there is a mathematical algorithm for unlocking a combination lock?"

"I suppose you could go with the logical approach." He smiled. "I go on instinct."

"And your instinct tells you magic is real?" she asked, taking a drink from her smoothie, but keeping her eyes on him as she drank. "Can you do magic?"

"I have amazed and impressed my friends with my stupendous magic."

"There's always a trick to it."

With a smile, he touched her cheek – she shivered a little – and put his fingers behind her ear. "What's that behind your ear?" He pulled out a quarter.

"That's the oldest one in the book."

"Perhaps, my dear, but still a classic."

"What does that have to do with anything?"

"It's magic."

"No, it's a trick."

Eric took out a dollar bill from his wallet. "Houdini

and Bess used to do a mind-reading act together. In order to achieve the desired effect, they had a series of code words that represented numbers and letters. If I wanted you to read my mind and tell me the serial number on this dollar bill, I could ramble off a series of secret words, giving you hints, and it would appear as if I were talking about the weather or whatever, but secretly giving you the numbers." Eric demonstrated, and Dawn tried to peek at the dollar bill, but he hid it from her. "Let's say the word 'pray' means number one, the word 'please' means number six, the word 'tell' is five, and 'now' means four. Got that?" She nodded, and he said, "Pray, now tell me please, what is the first four numbers on this dollar bill?"

Dawn smiled, thought about it, remembering the code words. "One, four, five, six."

"Ta da! You must be able to read my mind!"

"You've just proved my point. That's a simple trick."

"To you and I, we know how it worked. To a passerby, it's magic."

"But it's never real magic."

"How does understanding take away its power? You and I shared a secret, one only we understood." He shrugged, reached into his pocket, and pulled out Dawn's watch. "You want this back?"

She looked at her wrist. No watch. "How did you?"

"Magic!"

"That's not magic at all. That just makes you a pickpocket!" She snatched her watch and put it on, but she was smiling. He had gotten her with that one.

Eric pointed at her drink. "How's the smoothie? I've been wanting to try one."

"Very good. Very sweet."

"I like sweet too."

"I know. Marshmallows."

"My mom used to feed them to me, but mostly I just played with them, squished them, and built things with them. I said, 'Mama, did you shrink down the clouds?' and she said yes. I really believed her."

"That's sweet."

"That and licorice. Love that too."

"I like licorice," she said, very quietly with rose color to her cheeks, as if she were telling him the most personal of secrets.

"I have Jack 9 gum. It's licorice flavored. I like it better than the cinnamon one they make." He took a package from his knapsack which was on the floor beside him. He handed Dawn a piece. "For later," he said.

"Thank you." She put it in her purse. "It's old-fashioned," she said in the same whisper.

"What is?" He whispered too, mimicking her but not realizing it.

"Licorice. I like old-fashioned things."

"Me too."

"Really?" Eyes bright.

He held up his pen.

"Oh yeah." She smiled and shyly ate a Frito, trying to quiet the crunch.

"I collect a lot of old things actually. I love that stuff."

"I collect dolls. Porcelain ones," she said, feeling a little embarrassed at having told him such a personal thing.

"How many do you have?"

She shrugged.

"Have you been in the Arlington? That's where I'm staying. It's very old-timey. You'd probably like it."

"I haven't yet but I want to. Al Capone used to stay there. This guy at work is doing his research on Capone."

A little twinge of jealousy hit Eric at the mention of

another man. "Yeah? I'm not really a big fan of gang-sters." He finished off his sandwich, took a long drink. "They have good food at the Arlington though. You should come by for dinner one night."

Whatever the reddest of red could be, if red could blush, Dawn's face went that shade. Her heart was no longer merely warmed, it was flooding and beating and pumping, so hot. That little pilot light was glowing. A man at a table near them took off his jacket, wondering why it had suddenly gotten so warm. A woman fanned herself with a napkin. The café window fogged over with a fine mist.

"I had some wonderful cornbread dressing the other day," he said. Eric was not trying to entice her, or woo her, he was merely stating what he believed to be the obvious – we should have dinner together; it is only natural and right. "I'll perform some magic for you."

"A rabbit out of a hat?" It was the only thing she could think of to say. She wanted to scream "Yes, I'll have dinner with you!" but also wanted to run back to the train car in the woods, safe with her daydreams and dolls. It was like winning the lottery. What am I suppose to do now?

Playfully, Eric sighed. "That is such a cliché. Rab-bit out of a hat. Please. Is that what you think of me? My magic is stupendous!" He put his hand over her hand, and on instinct, she jerked it away. His face grew soft, a little confused. "Really good apple pie at the hotel." His voice was so quiet.

"Did you know if ripe apples are on the tree at the same time as the blossoms then it means someone will die. My landlady told me that." Quiet too.

Eric was taken aback. What an odd thing to say. "That's silly."

"Yeah, I know. She's a little weird."

He smiled, wanted to reach for her hand again, but

stopped himself. "The only complaint I have is the wine they serve at the hotel. We can always bring our – " The words spoken made him realize it instantly.

"Corner Wine?" she asked, knowing.

"I'm sorry. I didn't mean ... some people like – "

"Sour? That's suppose to be part of its charm." She ate a few Fritos and added, "You don't have to apologize. It's not my wine. It's my family's company. My family's creation. I didn't want it, so I sold it."

"Why didn't you want it?"

"It's sour."

Eric smiled. Understanding. "Makes sense." He drank the last of the Sunkist, then added, "And now you're out here in Hot Springs having lunch with a Houdini affi-cionado aka stalker who professes to have stupendous magic and what would the family think of that?"

Dawn smiled, opened the candy bar. "Nothing. They're all dead."

Eric stopped smiling. "Oh. I didn't realize you meant ... I'm sorry to hear that."

"I'm not." She meant it to be shocking. Eric was indeed shocked and reached for a marshmallow to hand her, but he cupped it in his palm instead. It flattened in his hand. He contemplated saying nothing but could not resist, his heart filled always with thoughtfulness. He ate the marshmallow, then put his hand over her own again – that feel of warm so strong, and he pressed down on it, holding it there. "You'll see them again," he said. "Don't worry."

"What?" She tried to pull her hand away.

"No one really dies." He squeezed her hand. His voice had the same gentle confident tone as his grand-mother's when she had told him about death. Eric meant well, but he had no concept of what Dawn was feeling. For all his insight and intuition, his reliance on instinct, the kind of pain that Dawn felt was as foreign to him as computer slang would be to a silent film star. Not only was it jargon, there was no frame of reference. Without realizing it, he had just said the worst possible thing to this damaged soul. He had thought he told her life was eternal, but what she heard was that she would never be free, never be safe.

Flustered, Dawn said, "I saw them all put in the ground. They were quite dead."

"Their bodies maybe."

She yanked her hand from his and looked at the clock. Dawn was like a moth emerging from the cocoon, one drop of rain, and she recoiled back inside. "I need to be getting back." She rubbed her hand as if it had been burned. It needed to be doused with cold water. It would hurt later but feel better.

"Stay a little longer. You won't be late. The museum's only a few blocks up." This handsome man of gentle soul with insight and love so deep that he filled books upon books did not understand her reaction, but she had to emerge from the cocoon eventually. A butterfly was waiting. But the look she had in her eyes was more than just fear. It was downright fright, as if the dreadful act had already occurred.

"I really should go."

"I wish you wouldn't."

In her haste, she spilled the strawberry smoothie. It rushed toward his notebook, staining it before he could grab it. "I'm so sorry," she said. Eric shook off the liquid. "Did I ruin it?" Eric said no. She grabbed a bunch of napkins to help wipe the pink stain. She saw one phrase written in his journal: *Rosabelle, sweet Rosabelle, I love you more than I can tell.*

If she had been a baby bird, it was as if someone had pushed her out of the nest too early. She tumbled fast toward the ground. "I really have to leave," Dawn said, feeling crushed.

Eric tried to catch her, grab her arm, before she walked out. "Dinner?"

She stuttered, looking for an answer.

"You know where to find me, Dawn." Sunlight reflecting on his face. Genuine smile. Red-gold-then-orange ... growing inside a girl who had never taken root anywhere, had no connection to the soil.

Roots

Not knowing exactly where Third Street was, Eric jiggled the broken watch in his pocket and looked at the sign post next to him. Second Street. Close. Travis, the juggling boy from the café, had made good on his promise and had found the watch repair shop. Before walking on, Eric popped a piece of the licorice-flavored gum into his mouth and looked down Second, not much but a few fast food joints, modern clothing stores, and a Target. There was a large tree trapped within a cement-block fence to look decorative, but it was so crammed that its roots were jutting up through the sidewalk, scarred and chafed from footsteps. It needed somewhere bigger to grow. It's growth had been stunted like the hands of his watch. The leaves, turning for fall, seemed too small and did not blow in the breeze. Eric plucked one, a blend like the flicker in his eyes, and twirled it between his fingers. The wind caught it, blew it forward, and edged Eric onward.

The wind carried the echo of pop music from somewhere, the wail of a car alarm, and the repeat of a fast food order from a drive-through call-box. Eric wished he had his iPod, but took solace in the fact that his newspaper interview was over. The reporter had spoken so much that Eric wondered if she ever met a deadline. Her behind had been rooted at the bar of the Arlington for over an hour, and she had managed to ask him a variety of questions about his love life, but very few about his poetry, which Eric thought explained his passions perfectly. If any woman ever had the notion of what type of lover Eric Pilot would be, then they needed only to read his words.

"Some people say your poems are hard to understand. You like being ambiguous?" she had asked, pen in hand, ready to scribble his thoughts.

Eric had shrugged. He liked not doing interviews. "If it's ambiguous, it's because people are reading the poems word for word. Not feeling them as they were meant to."

"Ooh," she had cooed, wanting to devour him like a Creamsicle on a hot day. "That's very sexy."

"I'm not trying to be sexy, just honest."

"Then what *are* you feeling when you write? They are *love* poems after all." She had uncrossed her legs, not very demurely, and added, "Very *erotic*-sounding *love* poetry."

"To put it simply, I'm thinking about the one girl." Eric had felt the cold metal of the watch in his pocket and thought time moved too slow. Whenever he looked at the clock on the wall, it seemed like the hands never moved.

Legs crossed, annoyed. "So it's true that Eric Pilot is taken?" Her tone was snippy, then she quickly composed herself, sounding like a Hollywood reporter on the red carpet, too sweet, too fake. "You've ruined it for all us hopeful girls out there. Who's the lucky one? What's her name?" But he did not answer, simply stood, shook her hand, and thanked her for her time. "Is it Rosabelle?" she had asked, not mystically. No reply.

As he had walked out of the hotel lobby, Eric's thoughts were rooted on Dawn. This is not to say that Eric, falling fast into love, knew just who Dawn was to be. He did not. The flicker of something red-gold-then-orange had burned him before, but his instincts were as alert as an air traffic controller monitoring every blip in the sky. Sometimes there are images that appear on the radar that cannot be ignored.

That biplane still circled the city, and it was still above him as he reached Third. A crossing guard, dressed in a bright orange reflector jacket, fanned herself with a handheld "stop" sign and smiled at Eric. He noticed shops going in one direction and a quiet community in the other. He started to head toward the shops when a moving truck rounded the corner. The writing on the truck read "Cosine Movers: The angle to take when moving." It made a quick turn, remarkably not toppling over, on an unassuming street. In the distance, a dog barked. Eric thought he heard someone whistle over the noise of the rumbling truck. Faced with two routes, Eric made his choice. Instead of going toward the shops, Eric walked to the quiet street. Not even realizing that Dawn Corner lived at the end of this street, Eric was drawn by nature like a bee knowing the route to a field of plants.

Outside the apartment, Mrs. Crumper, wearing a brightly-colored tunic, waved the moving truck into the drive like a airport runway attendant while Mitch wiggled on the ground, trying to scratch his back. Eric admired the red brick building with ivy up the sides. It looked like a film set, too perfect to be real. The complex stood next to white-washed modern buildings advertising exercise rooms, swimming pools, and two months free rent. Like Dawn, Eric would have chosen Mrs. Crumper's building too.

The crossing guard, who had quietly followed him, planted herself on the corner to wait for children who would need to cross the street soon. "Lost?" she asked him.

He looked at the street sign. Eric paused, so motionless he could have been a quiet ghost; someone could have walked through him and neither would have flinched. Rahner. Bess Houdini's maiden name.

This journey, a book tour proposed at the last minute, led him to a street named Rahner and a café named Rosabelle ... and meeting Dawn, whose middle name was Beatrice. He shook his head ... in awe and in answer to the crossing guard's question.

The sun was starting to set, and Eric needed to find the watch shop before it closed. On the phone, they had told him it could be fixed while he waited. He was unsure of that, but trusted that for all his knowledge about the mystical passage of time, he knew nothing of the mechanics of watch-making. Eric gazed down the road a moment longer, then took out his watch, flipped it in the air like a quarter, and it landed back in his palm, face side up. Eric walked back down Third in the other direction. Time to get the hands of his watch moving again.

No matter how hard Dawn tried, she could not get the feel of Eric's touch off her hands. It was as if it had taken root like a weed, crawling up her skin like the ivy on the side of Mrs. Crumper's building. Vigorously, Dawn scrubbed her hands in the museum employee-only bathroom. The vine kept growing. She sighed and took stock of everything she had learned and tried to make sense of it, add up the clues like a detective, but she was adding it up all wrong. She was trying very hard to make two plus two equal five. She took a paper towel and dried her hands, leaning against a stall. In her head she computed, Eric was not staying in Hot Springs and he loved "more than he could tell" someone named Rosabelle. Dawn was smart enough to realize that was the name of the café, but that was obviously a coincidence. Why would he write "I love you more than I can tell" about a café? What was he doing in Hot Springs anyway? She had never asked him that. He had to be in town on business, writing in his notebook, the last stop, staying in a hotel. Was he an advertiser? Had he written a jingle for the café? None of that seemed to make sense. Rosabelle had to be a girl. Maybe he was a magician? That made sense. He performed magic and liked Houdini. In town for a show. He had an engagement on Saturday. Still, it did not explain Rosabelle.

In her stomach, the food she had eaten for lunch wanted to come up. She tried to hold it down, the strawberry smoothie, corn chips, and turkey all sitting heavy in her stomach. She almost lost her balance walking out of the bathroom. At her desk, she took the piece of gum Eric had given her from her purse. She popped it into her mouth and chewed. Did he – Eric! – taste like licorice? His name still sounded good too. Eric's list of good things had yet to be shaken. They all added up correctly. The bad list was a hard equation and she feared what "X" equaled. What would it solve anyway? Things like this always rolled around in Dawn's mind, coming quickly, leaving quickly. In and out and backwards and forwards. Over and over without a solution until she gave up and moved on. Dawn spit the gum out.

Her clear nail polish was peeling from the all the hand washing, and she scraped it with the X-Acto knife and listened absentmindedly to the other employees as they talked, waiting for the clock to chime five.

"It's haunted, I'm telling you," Will said.

"Oh, here it comes," said another worker.

"What?" asked the woman with the infomercial

hairdo, not really caring but happy to be distracted from work.

"Ghost story." If there had been a flashlight in his hand, Will would have stuck the flashlight under his chin, gathered everyone close, and told the story campfire-style. "A long time ago ... at the Grace Theatre, a magician asked a girl to come on stage, a little help from an audience member, you see. The trick was to make her vanish, you know, poof! She stepped into the box, razzle and dazzle, but ..." He paused, letting the perceived drama sink in. "She never repoofed." He slapped his hand hard against the table, making Dawn jump. In a whisper, Will added, "Disappeared. Forever. She haunts the place."

"We've all heard that story," said the infomercial woman. "Everyone knows she was probably having an affair with the magician, and they ran off together. It's the perfect cover."

"Ah-ha, but you admit that something *did* happen. It *did* take place," Will retorted.

"I think it's good publicity to get people back to the theater on Friday nights."

"Go and find out for yourself."

No takers.

"Gotta believe in magic," Sledge said, coming into the room, looking at Dawn.

"Really?" asked one employee, annoyed the janitor took a turn in the conversation. "If you look through the newspaper archives, we work in a museum and have such things at our disposal, you'll find several stories about the missing girl, who her father claimed was preggers, running off with the magic man, who vanished too, coincidentally."

"She haunts the place," Will said.

"She does not."

"No."

"Creepy." One believer.

"You're crazy."

"What do you think, Dawn? You're archiving materials on one of the greatest magicians who ever played at the Grace Theatre," asked Will, the only one aside from Sledge, who hadn't treated her like wallpaper, but they all looked anyway, and she wanted to sink inside herself. Out. Although Dawn wished she could will the hands on the clock to move, even she noticed it was an odd coincidence they were all discussing a magic show.

"I don't believe in ghosts," she replied. Defensive. Dawn stood up, pretending to look for something in a cabinet. Their eyes were no longer on her, but the feel of Eric's touch was still on her hand, the warmth and the way he had held it down heavy like a mound of dirt.

Having made his closing arguments about the vanishing girl, Will walked over and touched Dawn's shoulder. She jerked her arm away. "Whoa! Sorry," Will said. "Didn't mean to spook you. I was just going to say that you should go to the Grace Theatre, since you're doing the Houdini stuff. Yeah, I've done a lot of research on that theater. Big shootout there – Capone – pow pow – at that place. We could compare notes, get together for lunch tomorrow and rap, you know."

"I like to eat alone."

Will shrugged; Sledge watched quietly at the door and said, "Man, leave that girl alone. You're scaring her with the ghost stories." Will went back to his desk, unperturbed, and started packing up for the day. Sledge came over to Dawn and asked, "Are you feeling alright? You've been back and forth to that bathroom all day."

"I'm fine."

"Saw you at the Rosabelle today with your boyfriend."

"What? Oh, you mean, no, he's not my boyfriend."

"You looked like a couple to me."

"We're not."

"Should be," he said, looking her over. "Maybe that's why you're so upset." Before Dawn could respond, he moonwalked out the door. The nerve, she thought, of that man.

It was a few minutes early, but Dawn quickly gathered her things and left the building. Down the steps and out into dusk. There were a few stars, the moon too, trying to get settled into the night. The sun was slowly dipping below the horizon, ready for a nap. Dawn walked past the Rosabelle. Eric was not there. It was a strange thing about Dawn, her desire and her fear. They mixed, and not well, like snow and heat, one melting the other, then drowning the fire. It left her temperature lukewarm. Simply living. Not dead cold. Not fire alive.

As she made her way home, to hide like she had in her caboose, she repeated in her mind the mantra that she did not care to see Eric again anyway. A breeze blew dust into her face. She took off her glasses and wiped her eyes, making tears, washing out the dirt. With blurred vision, she stepped off the curb, nearly running into the fender of a Arlington Hotel shuttle bus. The driver honked his horn, yelled out, "Pay attention, lady! Watch where you're going!"

Irritated, Dawn ran the rest of the way home. In her yard, she flew past Mrs. Crumper, who was putting out licorice root to dry on a ramshackle table. She waved to Dawn, friendly-like. "Got your stuff today," she said but Dawn ignored her. The yard was littered with piles of leaves from Mrs. Crumper's earlier yard work. Mitch was peeing on Leon the Gnome again and looking up to the sky, as if he were watching a cloud as it drifted by. It looked extra white, like a puffy marshmallow, in the blue sky that was turning black for night. The dog howled.

A beautiful headboard, armoire, and nightstand

were out of place in her living room. Boxes were neatly organized and unopened, which Dawn thought was a little amazing thinking Mrs. Crumper would have nosed around in them. In the kitchen, more boxes awaited sorting. Stepping over everything, Dawn threw open each box, rummaging quickly, throwing things left and right, very much unlike herself. Everything out of order. She would regret this mess later. When she found what she was looking for, the smile that overcame her face was not like that of a pirate who found the buried treasure, but a sigh of relief like a patient receiving good news after an exam. From a box marked "kitchen utensils" she pulled out a meat tenderizer. It used to belong to her maternal great-grandmother (the one whose name was Beatrice), a Native American woman, who used it to make jerky to sale to travelers on their way to and from Oklahoma and Arkansas. Now Dawn was about to use it to smack her hand. Placing her right hand on the counter, she closed her eyes, counted backwards like the countdown to a rocket launch, and slammed the tenderizer against her hand as hard as she could stand. No bones cracked, no blood, but before morning a large bruise would form. This was how Dawn chose to solve equations that did not add up.

Order

Eric watched images in his mind like a child watching a parade, each thought a float with some ornate story, something to marvel at, something to enjoy. But the words came to him like a series of keys on a piano. He hit each one, paused, then played again, each word a note in music to match those floats on display in his mind. As it was when he was a child, the sound of words still made him happy. Alliteration. Juxtaposition. Nictitating. Words had rhythm. And Eric never wrote a word without meaning. The word "it," the letter "A," all placed with purpose, all in perfect balance, order – just like his philosophy on life. Every single word in a book, in a poem, in a lyric, they were all there for a reason. Each piece, each note, each letter, spelled one glorious feeling or thought ... and they sang. Take away one, the meaning is lost. Eric looked at the pattern of his life, all the little clues, the way they added up in the same way that he linked words in his poetry. Eric never tried to force two plus two to equal five. He watched the signs and did not fear the answer.

There were no signs of rain on this cheery-looking Wednesday morning. Eric pulled back the curtains of his

hotel room window. Bright sun. Blue sky. No clouds.
Meeting his soulmate was as sure as the sun coming up in
the morning. And there it was, as he looked outside, the
sun. Always there whether he looked at it or not. Even in
the dark sky. It was still there; he just couldn't see it.
Something, he believed with all his heart, he had set into
motion before he was Eric Pilot, boy from Alaska, famous
poet, America's most handsome.

    The little biplane still circled the city, high up in the
clouds. Eric took a sip of coffee, sat on the couch, looked
over some of the words he had written the night before.
Like the cup of coffee he drank now, the drink existed because he had set the timer on the coffee pot before going to
sleep. Without any doubt, he knew there would be a full
pot of coffee in the morning. He planned it with one simple motion. *He* planned it. Before he had slept, he created
what waited for him when the sun arose.

    The same was true for every word of his poetry.
The same was true for meeting Dawn.

    Dawn saw a pattern in her life too. It was like the
alphabet; she knew the order from beginning to end, always
the same. And, like the alphabet, in sequence alone it
spelled nothing.

    She wrapped a bandage tight around her hand and
left for work, running a little late. The Rosabelle was
crowded, but Eric was at his regular spot by the window,
drinking orange juice and eating a piece of Mrs. Sunshine's
Crumb Cake. Dawn learned early on to enter and leave a
room like the wind. She was only a breeze that you felt,
never knowing exactly where it came from, or its destination. Quiet. Invisible. But Dawn was not transparent like
the wind, especially in Eric's eyes, nor did she really want
to be, and the bell above the door – ding-ding – signaled
her arrival like an alarm announcing morning.

He smiled. "Breakfast?"

"I have to go to work."

"See you at noon then?"

"Do you work here?"

He laughed. "No."

"Do you work for the Rosabelle, the company that owns it?"

"No."

"Are you an advertiser?"

"Why do you ask that? I'm a – "

"Are you a magician?"

His eyes widened. "Not really. I'm a – "

She had stepped inside to see if the pattern of her life had been rearranged. Dawn felt stupid and walked back out, muttering curses internally. Through the window, Eric watched Dawn walk down the street, admired her legs, the swish of her hair in the breeze. He watched her like a cat, quietly stalking, watching with a singular thought in mind. He even imagined the clack of her heels on the pavement, although he thought to himself, she never really made such a clack. She really was quiet like a mouse, but today he could almost hear the smack of her shoes on the pavement.

As she made her way to work, an idea came to her. Oblivious, Eric waited.

At his table in the Rosabelle, Eric spent the morning quietly writing in his notebook. While he was sufficiently caffeinated by the time noon rolled around, the day had droned on, time stuck like a dab of butter in molasses. Eric's watch was now perfectly synchronized with the clock on the wall. He saw his reflection in the watch glass. Any minute now. Eric ran his fingers through his hair and checked his shirt for lint. Tick tock. The little ding-ding of the bell above the door. Right on time. He knew she would be back, but one thing was not part of Eric's plan and a whip of jealousy struck him hard, nearly knocking the wind out him. If he had been that biplane that still circled the sky, he would have dropped with a thud as if his wings had been clipped mid-air. He shoved his watch back into his pocket.

"This is Will from work, the one doing the Capone research," Dawn said. Her eyes played a cruel game, held something sharp to cut him down. I don't need you. I don't really like you. Not really. The flicker in Eric's eyes went white hot. He had never expected to wake up to a coffee pot that had boiled over. The rage in his eyes shot through Will, but unaware that he was a pawn in Dawn's mean game of jealousy and fear, Will smiled wide. Eric shook Will's hand reluctantly.

"Hey, wait a minute – are you ... no freakin' way ... oh my gosh, you're ... no, are you Eric Pilot?" Will asked, excited. "I love your stuff, man!" He wouldn't let go of Eric's hand, kept shaking it.

"What stuff?" Dawn asked.

"Wait 'til everyone at work hears about this. Eric freakin' Pilot!" Will flopped down in a seat at the table and started to talk rapidly, but neither Eric nor Dawn listened. Eric stood, pulled out a chair for Dawn.

Will rapped the table with his hands. "Why didn't you tell me, Dawn? He's one of my favorite writers! Awesome!"

"Writer?" Dawn whispered, taking the seat, feeling Eric behind her, pushing in the chair. How did that fit into the equation? What did that spell? Maybe Rosabelle wasn't real? A character in a story? A play? A poem ... please not a poem, she thought, that might make her real. Eric sat across from her as before, his regular spot. Curiosity, not courage, made her look into Eric's eyes. Something different in his eyes. The light that flickered was not warm like a fireplace or hot like steaming coffee. It was not love or lust but anger. She had succeeded. He was jealous. Very much so. What she hadn't expected was to see sadness. That part she did not plan.

People always describe jealousy as the color green, but Dawn liked that color. It seemed fresh and alive and friendly. Like Dawn had already told Eric, the grapes on the vine were always green first, but when it was time, they were forced into alcohol, a substance that gave people a false sense of joy. Jealousy was much like that, a dark substance that flowed smoothly down the throat, but left you with a headache, an emptiness. Dawn had spent more than her fair share of days being jealous. She wished, if she could, to be a leaf, never having to grow into anything other than a leaf, never to be forced into wine, or jam, or anything other than a living thing enjoying the sunlight and each day. But the edges of Dawn's leaf – Eric! with the long list of good qualities – were turning brown before her eyes. She didn't want to hurt him, just push him away so she would not get hurt. Many times she had felt that terrible sense of loss. Jealousy curls its victims into a ball of hate and anger and fear. Like a bubbling volcano ready to blow, all you can think of is obliterating everything, letting the heat roll over everything, destroy it, leave nothing behind. Charred and burned.

Eric felt this now. His passion so great already that he wanted to leave a path of scorched ground, nothing but ashes in its path. But Eric had never experienced jealousy the way Dawn had, because Eric rarely fought for any girl he wanted. When he came into the picture, Eric was like a hero rushing onto the movie screen, he knew he would be victorious. Women swooned and fell at his feet, but if any man ever did challenge him, if any girl glanced away from his gaze, then Eric felt pangs of anger so deep that he found it hard to remain in control. He would clutch his fist, bite his lip, anything to keep from snapping back. It didn't take much to set this feeling into motion.

"You're wearing a new perfume," he had once said to a girlfriend. "Did someone buy that for you?" She had told him no, but the suspicious seed had been planted and took awhile to uproot.

For Dawn this was different. Dawn never won. She expected to be jealous. There was always another girl, a prettier girl, a girl who did not have an odd piece of hair jutting out the side of her head. The object of Dawn's affection never reciprocated. But here sat Eric with that same hurt in his eyes. She glanced away, then felt Eric touch the bandage on her hand. Even in anger, his tender spot could not be hidden. Very gently, he hooked a finger underneath the bandage, pulled it back to glimpse the bruise.

"What happened?" Eric asked.

Dawn stammered, "I hurt myself moving furniture."

"You need help, Dawn?" he asked, protective, grabbing her hand again, holding it perhaps a bit too long. Warming. She did not move her hand away.

"I'm fine," she said. His words were kind and honest. She heard that in his tone. Eric's words, this she was beginning to think, could be trusted. The little volcano in him receded, calmed down. He would not burn her.

"So, yeah, I'm thinking, yeah, I could have been a poet too, because I've written a lot of stuff," Will rambled on. "And, you know, the lifestyle is freakin' awesome. Lounging at home in your pajamas, yeah man, just typing, sleeping 'til noon."

"I don't sleep 'til noon." Terse. It was a hint of something Dawn had yet to hear in Eric's kind voice.

"I'm just saying, you know. The writing like you do, I bet you get a lot of wacko girls in love with you. Yeah, that would be awesome."

"No. It is not."

Dawn smiled at Eric's comment. Will had nothing left to say, as if all the helium in a balloon had seeped out. He got like that a lot, overly excited, then he shriveled up once the energy dissipated. Dawn took the momentary lapse in his rambling to redeem herself. Her plan had been a terrible idea. It was out of order like a stack of papers thrown into the air. She wanted to make a neat stack, put everything back together, because not only did she cause Eric pain, but hurting him felt worse than any pain she had felt. "He's helping me with some of my research," she said to Eric. "Houdini played the Grace Theatre, and Will has a lot of research about the old theater because Capone had a shootout there."

"I'm working on a book," Will said, thinking Eric would be impressed. Will's helium was replenishing quickly. "About Capone. I'm hoping to get an Associated Press article, set me up as an expert in the field, then put it all into a book." He leaned back in his chair, hands behind his back. "Make me some money, buy me an island, and live with the Tiki torches and a Brazilian supermodel." He pointed at Eric. "I bet you make a lot of bank."

"I live in the same house I grew up in," Eric replied.

"Dawn has to get down to the Grace Theatre. It's haunted. See, they had this magic show – "

"I don't think Houdini is haunting – " Eric started.

"Not Houdini, this other magician." He recounted the tale to Eric. "So anyway, yeah, they're bringing the magic shows back on Friday nights. First show this weekend. You can see for yourself."

"I don't believe in things like that," Eric said.

"Are you kiddin' me? Really? With the stuff you write?" Will said.

Dawn looked at Eric, wanting so badly to read his words. If his notebook had been opened on the table as before, she would have dared a glance. Even if ... just to know.

Eric answered, "I believe in reincarnation, living again, things of that nature – "

Dawn interrupted. "Is that what you meant yesterday about ... seeing family again?"

"Yes. Not ghosts. Is that what you thought?"

"I don't believe in ghosts." But she didn't like the idea of reincarnation that much either.

"I'd totally haunt people," Will said.

"There's no point in that to me. Roaming around? Why?" Eric responded.

"I'd meet up with some other ghosts, cool ones like Mark Twain, and get into some mischief," Will said.

"Not Capone?" Eric's voice was growing softer, less terse. Will was starting to amuse him.

"Can't imagine he'd be all that nice. He's an interesting character, but he's freakin' dangerous." Will pondered for a moment, then added with a sigh and rub of his stomach, "Man, I'm so freakin' hungry."

"Lunch on me," Dawn said to further redeem herself.

"I can't let you do that," Eric said, standing and taking out his wallet. "What can I get everyone?"

"You're the best, man," Will said and ordered a ham and cheese with a pickle on the side. "They serve Prickles Pickles here. Those are the best. Imported from Fate, Alabama."

Dawn did not bring her lunch from home that day. She had fixed it, but lost in her confusion about Eric, she had left it on the kitchen counter. "What you had yesterday looked good, but can I have cheese on mine?"

"You can have whatever you like," Eric said with a smile. "Swiss or cheddar?"

"Swiss."

While Eric placed the order, Dawn went to the bathroom and looked at the bruise on her hand. It was ugly.

She was embarrassed Eric had seen it. She ran water over it to reduce the swelling then re-wrapped it. When she came back, Eric and Will were carrying the food over to the table.

Will stuffed his face immediately, not waiting for the others. "You know, we should have invited Sledge. Yeah, everyone at work thinks he's oddball, but he can jam like nothing else!"

"Who's Sledge?" Eric asked, the jealousy monster whispering in his ear with a snicker.

"He's this cool cat at work who has like this freaky-ass sixth sense or some jive. He told me I'm going to fall in love with this red-haired chick. I haven't met her yet but I'm still looking. Yeah, so anyway, Sledge freakin' loves, worships, all things Motown. He plays down at the MJ Music Box sometimes, jams with different bands that come to town. On Saturday, he's sitting in with this swing, rock-type, funked-out something-type of band that I hear is the best. Yeah, you should check him out."

"He's the janitor," Dawn explained.

Eric nodded cool-like. "Musical janitor. Dig it."

With mouth full, Will added, "There's some dude in town, some pilot, he's sitting in with 'em too. Plays harmonica. It's gonna be sweeeeet."

"Friday night magic shows, bands on Saturdays. Sounds like a great weekend. Good thing I'm staying through it," Eric said, giving Dawn a long stare; she cast her eyes away, looked out the window, didn't want him to see her smile. A leaf rolled down the sidewalk back toward the Grace Theatre and the MJ Music Box.

"The main drag is jumpin'." Will said through bites of his sandwich. "You know what would be sweet? Oh, man, this would be sick, you play any instruments? I bet they'd let you come on stage too, being famous and all."

Famous? Dawn thought. She had not thought of

that. He was famous. As soon as they had walked in, Will had recognized Eric. Did other people know him too? Did Eric think she knew? He couldn't. She had asked about his job that morning. He did not seem offended. She was not a big reader and would not know the name of a poet, famous or not. In that moment, Dawn's heart sank again. He wasn't just a handsome man from a train, a writer, visiting Hot Springs for a short time, who liked marshmallows and not cheese. He was some sort of celebrity, truly and really out of reach. Rosabelle was probably a Brazilian super-model. Again, she tried to make two plus two equal five. She ignored his stare, the obvious fact he was asking her out, that he had already asked her to dinner. Dawn was like a boat in a heavy fog, Eric the lighthouse, but she ignored his bright light, thinking only of the dark clouds hovering over the water.

"I don't play any instruments," Eric said in answer to Will's question. "But, I tell you what I wouldn't mind doing. I wouldn't mind having a look at the museum's Houdini materials. I have an extensive collection of Houdini memorabilia myself. Do you think the museum would mind if I stopped by to look around?"

"That would be awesome!" Will said.

"I can ask," Dawn said. Glad to make Eric glad ... even if.

"Tomorrow before lunch?"

"What about Mrs. Lawley?" Dawn asked Will. "Do you think she'll – "

"Lookit, let me tell you something about Mrs. Lawley, she ain't nothing. Her position is purely a courtesy. Besides, she'd be thrilled to have a famous writer ogling the collection."

"I won't ogle. And I won't touch," Eric said, his hand was very close to hers. As always, that constant flicker in his eyes ... and she was mesmerized. Just as planned ...

Constant

Dawn was like a hypochondriac in a doctor's office, knowing there would be bad news. Dawn believed everything with Eric would end in heartache, but she felt drawn to him like a child entranced by a burning match. Like a pilot to flight. She was also slightly mesmerized by the erotic poster Mrs. Crumper had on her wall. Inside the landlady's house was much like the outside; it looked like an English cottage straight from a fairy tale with the exception of that poster and a poorly made dragon sculpture on the kitchen counter ... at least Dawn thought it was a dragon, even though it appeared to be missing legs. Absentmindedly, she watched Mrs. Crumper sip licorice root tea. Dawn was aware that Mrs. Crumper was talking rapidly, but her thoughts were elsewhere. Her feelings for Eric were becoming as clear as a lucid dream. At what point, she wondered, will it become a nightmare? Her plan had been simple – move to Hot Springs and sit among boxes of old things, examine, catalog, shelve, and preserve quietly. Freedom! Nothing more. Certainly not love. Is that what it was? You can't love someone that quickly, she reasoned.

"'Fraid the house is on fire," Mrs. Crumper said, pouring another cup of tea and noticing Dawn was lost in thought. "Aliens have landed. Apparently in your apartment. They said they want to swipe your knickers."

"I'm sorry. What?"

"S'all right. I've had my share of daydreams. Daydreams, yes, usually involve a young man. Am I right?" To her, Dawn was a little blanket of clouds covering the sky, but she could see a faint halo of light peeking through it. She patted Dawn's bandaged hand, but politely ignored how it had happened. Dawn did not respond to the touch, so lost in her thoughts she was.

"No. No, I was thinking about work."

"Hmmm, didn't look like a work fantasy to me." She winked and picked up a newspaper on the chair beside her. There he was. "Eric Pilot!" the landlady exclaimed.

Eric. That name.

To say that little miracles don't happen would be a lie. In her heart, Dawn prepared for the nightmare ... but then and there his photo appeared.

"Eric? He's in the paper?" Dawn asked, but this time Mrs. Crumper did the ignoring, staring at the photo like a giddy schoolgirl.

"I've always wanted a face to put with those words!" Mrs. Crumper said with her hand over her heart.

"You've heard of him?" Famous.

"Of course, I've heard of 'em. I love him. You don't?"

Yes. "I've never read his books."

"He writes the most romantic ..." Mrs. Crumper had to stop to sigh, for a moment lost in a fantasy herself. "Look here, he's having a book signing on Saturday." He was indeed quite famous. "Drat, Mitch has a vet appointment that morning. I'll never make it." She gently nudged Mitch, who was sleeping under the table. "What are the chances he'd get rabies. Eh? Better not chance it." Then she elbowed Dawn and tapped the paper. "I wouldn't kick him out for getting crumbs in the bed. I can see why he was voted one of the most handsome men in America."

"He was voted the most handsome man in America?" Very famous.

"You know how those magazines like doing those polls," she said, getting up to stoke a fire in the wood-burning stove in the corner. The little room was very hot. "Voted him most attractive writer. Can't say I disagree now that I've seen him." She sat back down, tapped the paper again. "Just look at those cheekbones! He's a dear. Very handsome indeed. Which is odd for writers. They usually aren't much to look at."

"What does he write exactly?"

"Love poetry. I've always had a crush on him."

"You just saw him."

"That's how good of a writer he is." She winked.

"May I?" Dawn asked so quietly that Mrs. Crumper barely heard her. She handed Dawn the paper. His "America's Most Handsome" photo looked back at her next to a headline that said "Pilot Brings His Passion to Hot Springs." Dawn read over the interview, memorizing the words like a computer, filing away his quotes to pull up later and analyze, maybe save some for a daydream.

Nightmare.

Dawn put the paper down. "He has a girlfriend."

With a raised eyebrow, Mrs. Crumper said, "Is that what it says?"

"He dedicates every book to a girl named Rosabelle." For Dawn, life went on without emotion, as usual. She was awake. Clouds in the sky. It would most likely rain.

It was more than a sliver of light that Mrs. Crumper saw through the clouds. There was a hailstorm forming inside

Dawn. Everything in the kitchen seemed quiet. Mitch snored. On the wall was a cuckoo clock, and it tick-ticked back and forth. Click click. Mrs. Crumper tap-tapped her foot. Clack clack. She could not hold back, and said with another raise of her eyebrows to see if Dawn would look up, "That's the great mystery about Eric Pilot."

"What?" Dawn said back, terse.

"About Rosabelle. There are theories, of course, about who she is."

"I really don't care," Dawn said, wiping her mouth, getting ready to leave. The room was too hot. "I don't keep up with celebrity gossip."

"No one knows who she is exactly." In a comforting way, she added, "Some people think it might be his mother or his grandmother."

"He writes books of love poetry and dedicates them to his mother? That's a little unlikely."

Mrs. Crumper shrugged, stood up, and left the kitchen. When she returned, she held a book with a leather cover made to look worn. It gave no indication that it was a modern book, produced by a large publishing house. It had no fancy dust jacket or author's giant photo emblazoned on the back. She handed it to Dawn. Delicately, Dawn held it in her hands as if she were examining it with white gloves at work, as if the book were a valuable document. In many ways it was. These were Eric's words. White pages, yellowed deliberately, gold embossing down the sides, each page held a poem.

"He'll make you a believer," Mrs. Crumper said.

Dawn was hesitant. "A believer in what?"

"Magic."

"I thought he wrote love poems?"

"He does," she said with a smile. "Go on, now. Take it. Keep a glass of cold water beside you as you read, love. I swear they use flame retardant paper to print that man's words. Can't imagine what kinds of things he'd say in person."

The first page, Dawn saw it, dedicated to Rosabelle. She wanted to be alone now more than ever.

Grumpy, Eric flipped channels on the television. He couldn't figure out why he was so irritable. Maybe it was the looming storm. It rains too much in Arkansas; he cursed it internally. He was starting to feel like Dawn, damned little black cloud every time you turned around. But, Dawn no, he did not think of her in a negative way at all. His jealousy for Will had receded; Eric knew Dawn was a little cactus with many spines to protect herself. He wrapped his blanket around him – he swore the scent of her sugary perfume still lingered on it after the train ride – and watched a local commercial advertising Friday night's magic show at the Grace Theatre. It was shown during every break, a corny advertisement shot against a green screen with lots of flashy graphics nearly yelling "Don't Miss It!"

Eric turned the television off and lit a fire. The room wasn't warm enough. He became bewitched by the flicker. Rising, crackling, shades of orange. He calmed a little. Rummaging around in his knapsack, he pulled out his journal and looked at the last entry, which read, "Who is this frightened girl with bright face covered in night?" Quickly, he jotted down, "Dawn Corner. She doesn't know who I am. Doesn't like magic." He put the journal down, searched around in one of the traveling trunks and threw things askew, mostly books, left and right. Collections by John Keats, e.e. cummings, and Rumi. A book by Octavio Flemming. The Houdini bio. His tattered copy of Richard Bach's *The Bridge Across Forever* was held together with tape – one of his favorite love stories. He thumbed through it, closed his eyes, and thought about Dawn. He needed a sign for his next step. See, Eric believed it was possible to find the answer to any question, cosmically mystically, by opening a book at random. With eyes closed, he pointed to the word "theater." Eyes open. Eric shook his head, and muttered to himself with a smirk, "Doesn't always work."

Eric could not shake a negative cloud surrounding him, even though he was excited at the prospect of seeing Dawn's Houdini materials at the library. Unable to sit still, he put out the fire, grabbed a light jacket, and headed out the door. With the chill in the air, Eric huddled into himself, hands in pockets, slumped over looking like a man who had been on the road too long with his windswept hair (he had left his fedora in the room) and his jacket with an ink stain on the sleeve. Like he had told Dawn, being from Alaska, cold weather did not normally bother him, but there was a dark vibe in the air. Anger. Suspicion. Thunder. Why? He jumped back at the sound of the thunder, cracked a twig as he stepped on it, then kicked it into the street.

Out of habit, he went straight to the Rosabelle first, but they were locking up for the night. The waitress, who still had a glimmer of hope in her heart, waved to him. He quickly waved back and turned around, walking back toward the Grace Theatre with its old-fashioned marquee from another time. He was about to cross the street and head back to his hotel when a strange little thing happened then – as so often happens in stories of love – it started to rain, but in the chilly autumn air the rain was warm. Warm, Eric thought. He looked at the sky and the little cloud wasn't rumbling with fury. It appeared to be weeping, slowly changing to white as it released its burden of tears. The warm water poured over his face, ran down his neck, his chest ... to his ... There was thunder, sure enough, but to him it sounded like the clap of a hand.

"You want to come inside, out of the rain?" Travis asked, perfectly placed behind the Grace Theatre ticket window, seeing Eric getting wet. He had just sold a ticket for Friday's show to an elderly couple and was closing up for the night. "Friday's tickets are selling like cracker jacks, man. It's a constant stream of magic lovers," Travis said, unlocking the front door to let Eric inside. The theater kept its historic-landmark feel with maroon carpeting on the floor and curtains with gold tie-backs that led to the stage.

"Do you always work the ticket window?" The idea came quickly like a muse moving a poem.

"Whatever razzle dazzle they need, I'm cool," Travis said, putting on a yellow fedora, ala Dick Tracy.

"Are you working Friday?"

"O' course, that's the big show. They're rehearsing now. You want to look around?"

"Don't you need to be getting home? Don't you have school tomorrow?"

Travis shrugged. "I'm a night owl."

Eric smiled, patted Travis on the back.

"How's your pocket watch? Did they fix it?" he said, taking Eric on a tour.

"Yeah, it's good. But, I've got another job for you."

Dawn took a sip of the fuzzy navel, wrapped her robe tighter around her waist, and sat down on the couch, which had no cushions because she, swept in fury and pain, had thrown them on the floor. Her own little thunderstorm. Only moments before the apartment had been a strange mixture of new and old with the furniture arranged. Now it looked like a tornado swirled through uprooting the antique coffee table, turning over the iPod dock, and kicking over a new armchair made to look old. The dolls were unharmed on an oak bookcase. The flat screen television remained intact and on. Dawn didn't know why she had a television anyway; she rarely watched. It seemed like something everyone had to have – like windows, the view never changed. But she watched now, letting herself get caught up by FoodWorks chef Faith Orion making a crumb cake with a marshmallow topping. Dawn could go for something sweet to wash down the anger, wash away her feelings for Eric, but doing that would be like bathing away sand in the waves of an ocean. There's always a little grittiness left and she knew that. Mostly she wanted to ignore her feelings, pretend they weren't there. The numbness. She needed that. She damned herself instead, sat through a local commercial for the magic show on Friday, and felt a little twinge in her heart. She had to go there. For work, she said to herself. Not magic. Not Eric. Not with Eric ... the man with a girlfriend. Damned Rosabelle ... who was probably a model. Famous men always dated models, but Eric seemed too smart to be that stupid.

For a moment Dawn sat in silence after she turned the television off. She could search the internet and find out information about him. Instead, she reached for Eric's book of poetry ... dedicated "For Rosabelle." Dawn ignored that and decided to open the book at random, which she did not realize was profound. Dawn believed she had no question for an answer.

Constant. By Eric Pilot

The spine of the book did not crack when she opened it, not because Mrs. Crumper had read it over and over, but it was made like that – loose, open. The type of book you would cuddle with next to a warm fire. Much like Eric.

As she began to read, the lights flickered. Another storm. For a moment, she stared at the words on the page but listened to the raindrops hitting the metal rain gutter outside. Clink clink, then faster clink clink bang bang bang. As long as the lights stayed on, she would be fine. She lit candles throughout the room, just in case. And what was the harm, she thought, being drawn by unseen forces, in reading his words ... just for curiosity. She slid her hand down the spine seductively as if the book were Eric. To actually touch him again ... Again. If Dawn closed her eyes, she could perfectly remember the feel of his soft hands over her own. She looked under the bandage on her hand. Her bruise looked distorted like a small pool of candle wax. Wished she hadn't done it. Wished she wasn't the way she was. She returned to the poem in the book.

> *I am the fire in the distance.*
> *The constant state of arousal.*

She closed the book. Contemplating, Dawn looked around as if she were about to be caught in the act of something. With head down, she picked up a candle and took the book to her room. The bedroom was furnished now with her things. She kept the ornate mirror in its place, but the room had her large canopy bed. With the candle burning, the room felt completely old-fashioned. Dawn climbed beneath the covers, glanced at the rain-soaked window, saw the breeze blow the limbs on the trees, and pulled the covers around her. She looked small in her bed, almost like a little girl with her lacy nightgown and robe, but the thoughts consuming her mind were not those of a young girl. She opened the book again. This time she heard Eric's voice as she read. His voice started slow but sped up as she read, as if the words were racing to a conclusion as a flame ran up the page.

> *I am the fire in the distance.*
> *The constant state of arousal.*
> *Girl with mottled vision through frigid thought,*
> *See me, a light house. Glowing. You*
> *are cold like funeral black. You*

*desire to be warm, for your breath to be a fever. You
covet the flush on your skin. You*

"No," Dawn whispered. Eric's voice became more
seductive.

*will
melt at my touch, liquid and changed. You
Walk toward me. I
am the all-consuming fire. Desire. We*

We? Dawn wondered. Us.

*are
waiting
for You.*

Dawn put the book to her chest, slid deeper under
the covers. The room felt warm as if she were next to a
raging fireplace in the middle of summer. His voice
slowed.

*I will wait
even if certain You
will never come.
But I will always see You
in the distance,
a wind so swift,
brought by the currents of a storm, You*

Eric's voice raged. Thunder. Lightning.

*can fuel Me or destroy Me, but I
will always be the one
to Love You.*

Eric's voice quieted. The rain subsided. Stillness.

Dawn put his book to her lips, but did not kiss it. The look on her face was that of someone trying to decide the fate of another. She put the book on the dresser beside her, sunk deep into the covers, pulling them to her neck. Dawn glanced at the door; it was closed. Slowly, as if her actions would wake someone like stepping on a loose floor board in the middle of the night, she lifted her nightgown and very gently touched herself. In her mind, she felt Eric's hands, the feel of his fingertips, and where they touched her now. She could still hear his voice. *You will melt at* my *touch.* A tear rolled down Dawn cheek, as always when she did this, but this time it wasn't from shame. She wanted him more than any man, any fantasy, any lover she could conjure up in her mind.

Breathing humid air, Eric walked back to his hotel, hair still damp from rain, and enjoyed the steaming streets making fog in the night. Confident. Excited. Enjoying his little secret.

Dawn cried herself to sleep. The shame could wait until morning.

Secrets

It was a morning of secrets. Constant dreams of making love. Little whispers shared between lovers. Quiet. But, the night had been fitful too. Eric awoke every few hours with a sheer sweat covering his body like a sheen, the room feeling like an oven, covers tangled, pillow clutched in his hands underneath him. Eric felt that his own hands could never replace that of a woman's soft flesh. He found that self-gratification always left him feeling forlorn, but when he realized he was slowly grinding against the pillow as he thought about the dreams, he relinquished himself to pleasure. A few blocks away Dawn was burning her hand with a candle, Eric's book left on Mrs. Crumper's doorstep – to avoid temptation.

The world outside, as if it had slept through the night's raging-then-soft storm, awoke the same as always. Birds soared. Lights blinked. Crossing guards waited with their signs. Dawn re-wrapped her hand to cover the bruise and the burn, and Eric wrapped a scarf around his neck, grabbed his fedora, and headed downstairs. The morning air was crisp but sunny, and he would take his breakfast on the little open veranda/walkway of the hotel. Since it was an autumn weekday, the hotel was not very busy. It was the perfect place to meet in secret. He took a seat where he could watch a little trickle of water from one of the nearby springs casually meander past. The hotel was starting to look somewhat gothic, Halloween being a few days away. Along with orange and black streamers, there was a jack-o-lantern and a bail of hay in the lobby. A sign near it advertised the Day of the Dead festival at a nearby cemetery. No ghosts, Eric noticed. Most of the hotel staff had plastic pumpkins pinned to their uniforms. One such employee was stringing fake cobwebs near Eric on the veranda, unknowingly humming a song that Eric knew was about death. He felt a little shiver and took a sip of coffee. Halloween was not his favorite holiday. Ever since reading his first Houdini biography, Halloween always made him feel sad. Little Eric had borrowed, not purchased, the biography from a carney-style flea market huckster named Tag who roamed around the continent selling his wares and homemade whiskey. Eric had already spent all his allowance on gum, but noticing his interest in the book, Tag had told Eric he could read the book and return it on his next visit through Alaska. Keeping his promise, Eric did give it back, but had scribbled on the first page. He had confessed his sin, but Tag had only shrugged and added it back to his stash of used goods, ready to travel elsewhere and sell to another.

This year Eric was glad to be occupied during the holiday, especially meeting Dawn, but there was an odd pit in his stomach that ached and he didn't know why. He was starving though and layered a scone with grape jam. When he had studied at Cambridge in England, he ate scones with either grape jam or honey every morning, always outside, writing in his journal. At one point, he had contemplated staying in the country. He could mimic a British accent as spot on as Earl Grey tea. He had loved taking the black taxis and the double-decker buses. The cobblestone streets, red phone booths, and foggy evenings made him feel like he was always in a Sherlock Holmes novel. He had indeed loved the country, but when he left, he had told his friends that an American writer in Europe was a cliché (and not necessarily a good one). In reality it was his former beloved, having left him for Hollywood, that made him never return to England.

Those days were far behind him now. His life had moved rapidly after college. If he were to imagine those events scrolling by, it would move in quick notes like the morning news ticker on television. First book published at age twenty-three, international bestseller by age twenty-four, top-selling poet by age thirty. Eric had received just about every award a writer could acquire, even though some critics said his poems lacked "social relevance" and disliked his continual use of free verse. Those slights did not matter, because he was beloved by most critics and booksellers, but it was the romantics who kept his work in print. His words had been quoted, according to a website that kept up with such stats, more times in the past decade than all of his heroes, and most people recited his words at weddings, sent them as inspirational messages, and bought the rights for use in greeting cards, although the average person never recognized him walking down the street. Eric was glad for the general anonymity and flattered that his words touched people, but he wrote in hopes that one person would read and recognize him. Just that one. Surely, there would be a cosmic force that would draw her magically to his words. Maybe she would be perusing a book shop one day and just happen across his book? Maybe that book was out-of-place, put in with cookbooks, and she had come across it accidentally? Would she see the sign? He often wondered what she would be thinking when she realized he was talking about Her!

It was obvious Dawn had not read his books. Not even one. What did that mean? It did not matter, he reasoned. He would wait it out and see. Was he an advertiser? she had asked. Thinking back on that made Eric smile as he ate his breakfast. He savored the sweet jam for a moment, took a sip of coffee, and reached across to a vacant table to pick up yesterday's paper. There was his interview. He did not bother to read it, but caught the reference to "Rosabelle" aka "the big secret" in his life. He smeared a dollop of jam across his face in the picture. From the corner of his eye, he saw Travis approach and threw the newspaper back to the other table.

"I can't stay long. I have to go to school," Travis said to him, "but it's all set – "

"Shhh," Eric whispered, gesturing for him to sit down. Like spies involved in espionage, Travis enjoying it immensely, Eric spoke of secrets and thought of Dawn.

"To talk of things that lead to a kiss," Sledge quoted behind Dawn as he swept the floor. It was a verse from Eric Pilot. "I can't remember the next line. Something about simple words meaning more. You know this poem?" Dawn tried to ignore him, quietly answered no. "It's been in my mind all day," he said.

She sat at her desk, white gloves on, Houdini materials spread before her, and tried to concentrate on work, but secretly glanced at her watch. It was almost time. She had passed by the Rosabelle on the way to work but did not see him. In the front of her mind, his poetry lingered. She felt warm and agitated ... a little shame at seeing him soon. Would he sense what she had done while thinking of him? Would he know she had nearly molested his words, those poems of lust he had written for ... ? Now, in the back of her mind resided three other things, Eric had a girl named

Rosabelle, he was famous, and he was leaving town soon. It did not matter that he was on his way to see her. Everything tasted bittersweet like medicine sweetened with grape for children. To distract herself from the truth, Dawn left her desk and pretended to look for something, anything. Her hand hurt terribly – a bruise and burn. There were whispers all around her. She kept hearing his name, even though it was said quietly, voices and eyes directed at her. Why her? Who was she? The new girl? Or had she been there all along? Only Sledge noticed it was not odd that Dawn – not ugly, not pretty, a girl – was the flicker in Eric's eyes. Because Sledge could see too.

Barely five foot three, Dawn had to stand on her tip-toes to reach the highest shelf at the museum. She pulled down a stack of papers, stretching far up, and nearly fell backwards like she had on the train when she had tried to put her luggage in the bin (but this time it was all a ruse). Again, Eric was there to catch her. His fingers felt like a prickle of flame in her sides. She knew it was him without having to turn around. The room quieted, watching the scene, but his touch is not what first alerted her to his presence. It was his sweet woodsy maple scent. As soon as she had stood on her tip-toes, she had smiled and pretended to fall backwards. His lips, his breath with a scent of grape jam, were too close to her ear when he whispered, "Hi, Dawn." He said it like a secret, as if he had snuck in to steal away with her on some rendevous. But, of course, everyone in the room had seen him come in, and everyone watched as he strolled casually and cooly over to Dawn, as if he had predicted her fall and held his arms out, literally, a few seconds before she tumbled backward. It was as if he had been there to catch her (which of course he was) and not to see any documents at all.

When Dawn turned around to greet him, cheeks crimson, he kept his arms around her. He stroked her sides a little, tilted his head, and looked like he was about to kiss her. He wanted to. Their feelings were so blatant, so obvious, it was like a dark cloud signaling rain. The room was silent, watching, so quiet the telepathic whispers of these two were almost audible. Many years later, the museum employees would tell this story, far more entrancing than any old ghost story. They would claim, swear, that an actual arc of something red-gold-then-orange sparked between their chests, such was the power of this love.

With amorous dreams still fresh in his mind, and Dawn's fantasies still alive in her thoughts, they both suddenly became aware of their surroundings. Eric cleared his throat and stepped back. "Lovely museum," he said, looking around.

"Thank you," said Mrs. Lawley, sneaking up on him, startling him as if she had yelled in his ear unexpectedly. "I'm Ruth Lawley, head of the historical society patrons." She stuck out her hand, phony smile and all. She was as chipper as a chipmunk with a tree full of nuts, but Eric's first reaction was that the woman looked like a stick character drawn by an amateur without any knowledge of physical form or beauty. She had arms, legs, a dot for a head, and a crudely drawn dress that looked like a triangle on bottom and a box on top. Then he looked a little closer at her, looked into her eyes, seeing the real woman the way he usually did, and made her quickly turn away. A sad smile. She was lonely. Not in the same way that he felt Dawn's loneliness. Dawn could still be ignited. Mrs. Lawley was a piece of charcoal, used and burned. She was suicidal.

He wanted to say something kind, to cheer this sad woman up a bit, because he knew – and it was not vanity – that his words had a certain positive impact on women, but Dawn's hand accidentally brushed against his, and his thoughts returned to his real reason for being there. "I'm here to see what Dawn has to show me. Houdini – ”

Before Eric could finish, the woman with the infomercial hairdo came into the room, dropped a doughnut, and squealed like a teenager, “Is that Eric Pilot? Oh, geez, he’s even better in person!” People often spoke to him as if he were not in the room, talking about him in third person as if he were an oddity in a museum. Once he was even referred to as “it.” The woman eyed him closely without shame, almost nose to nose as if he were something in a glass case to be admired. Tap on the glass. “Now that’s a face! He, honestly, has the perfect male face.” She vigorously shook her head in disbelief.

“Amanda, please,” said Mrs. Lawley, shooing her away, a phony roll of her eyes in sympathy for Eric, but she did not make direct eye contact with him, which she would not do for the rest of the day.

“Eric, my man,” Will said, nodding rapidly. “Awesome.”

Eric ignored it all and took Dawn’s hand in his, squeezed gently. “Where’s your desk?” Dawn put the papers on a lower shelf, and could only point to her desk, her eyes locked with his eyes. That flicker in both. That arc.

Casually, Eric pulled out a chair for Dawn, took a seat himself. Before they could get started, Sledge walked over, asked simply, “To talk of things that lead to a kiss. What’s the next line? Been driving me nuts.”

Eric feigned remembrance and said in his eloquent voice:

> *To talk of things that lead to a kiss ...*
> *Mere simple words, magic and lust*
> *a spark of something gold between us, scarlet flush*
> *... words now ...*
> *hushed. Mean more,*
> *more*

Quiet to all
a scream to you. You hear me, my love,
as I shout across time.
To talk, yes, of things ... things that lead to a kiss.
Whispers. Secrets.
Unsure in the dark, be not afraid to speak.
The heat of our voices,
not air, not smoke, not fog,
impossible to vanish.
Fire, open mouths.
Eyes, golden light.
Two souls ... burning.
Wait. And Listen. Once more
for my voice. To kiss.
Kiss with magic and lust.

Not a single person in the room moved; they all listened and looked, waiting. Dawn Corner and Eric Pilot. Not a collection of genes, not physical, not a grouping of cells, not the product of upbringing. No, they were that arc. That spark. That flicker in the eyes. That whisper, he spoke of, in the dark.

"*Magic and Lust,*" said Sledge, the title of the poem.

Dawn rubbed her sore hand. For some reason, it did not hurt as much. Those words, she remembered, and these words she had just heard ... as if he had written them for her. Her! Maybe. She wiped a drop of sweat from her temple before it could roll down her face. Was Eric looking at her? She hoped not ... she hoped so ... much so ... so much. Just look. See. The fire in the distance. She could see it in his eyes. Her vision was not mottled. She could see. See me, Eric, she whispered then yelled in her mind.

Eric leaned his chair way back, resting on the two back legs – cool-like – the way a boy might do in a high school class, not paying a lick of attention to the teacher, plotting some after-school debauchery, but he was planning no such dealings, only thinking of one thing, one person. *I see you, Dawn.*

"You're a lovely writer," Mrs. Lawley said, clapping. The rest of the staff joined in.

Eric put up his hands, genuine embarrassment. He wished he had recited the poem in a whisper only Dawn could hear. "Can I see the Houdini stuff now?" he asked.

Mrs. Lawley would not let go, sidling up next to them, still unable to look him in the eye. "Now, tell us, Mr. Pilot, why is it that you're so interested in Houdini?"

"I like magic. My grandfather used to teach me card tricks." Had anyone looked beyond the celebrity in the room, they would have seen the real answer was a secret. Only one person was slightly aware, being an artist and being a bit more in tune, that something about Eric's answer did not ring quite true. Sledge tapped Eric's shoulder with his broom, gave him a knowing nod and walked out.

"Most of this stuff, it's just newspaper clippings, some ads, and a poster, " Dawn said as Eric looked over the things on the table. Very gently, she stopped him. "You'll need gloves too." She handed him a pair; the bandage underneath her glove was obvious.

"Your hand still hurt?" he asked, but he didn't touch this time, simply took the gloves, put them on.

She put her hand under the table. "A little." Mrs. Lawley, sans gloves, reached under some of the papers and pulled out a vintage poster advertising the show at the Grace Theatre – Houdini standing in chains with an insert of his hands holding a splayed deck of cards.

"Isn't this something," Mrs. Lawley said, feigning interest. In reality, Mrs. Lawley had voted against acquiring the collection, feeling the materials were too "pop culture."

Now that a well-respected writer was validating the items, she acted as if she had never felt any other way about it.

"If you don't mind," said Eric, noticing her avoidance of eye contact, "I would like to spend some time with my friend privately."

Another hush crept over the room and a bit of respect for his boldness. "I see," Mrs. Lawley said, standing properly, pretending not to be personally affronted. Dawn looked at Eric and smiled. He shrugged with a grin.

"Look, Eric," Dawn said, "here's the letter from Bess I told you about." The letter that people would talk about for years to come as it sat on display in the museum was nothing special. It was a simple letter from Beatrice Houdini thanking the manager of the Grace Theatre for a wonderful stay. Eric picked up the letter. For him, it was like a Rosetta Stone, maybe it had answers, maybe it was a key. For Eric, that moment, that little passing of a letter from Dawn's gloved hand, said much more. Dawn's voice was softer than ever, but she wanted it to be loud, wanted it to be a yell ... but only for him to hear. She had something that he wanted to see, almost like a secret to share. Her toes curled in her shoes, forgetting any jealousy any doubt.

"Wow," Eric said quietly – almost as quiet as Dawn's voice – after reading the letter. "She loved him."

"Who?"

"Bess. She loved Harry very much. They have a great love – "

"But that's not a letter to – "

"I know," he said with a friendly chuckle. He leaned in close to her, shutting everyone out, even Mrs. Lawley who still sat nearby – if she had been on the other side of a door, she would have placed a glass up to her ear to hear what was being said. "It's the love story that gets me, what fascinates me," he said.

Dawn shook her head. "The Houdinis?"

"Don't you know their story, Dawn?"

Something inside of her blossomed. They were close, very close. She could smell his sweet breath and the lingering taste of licorice. Her hand he took, the gloved one hiding a bandage, the little secret truth she hid, and he told her, "They had a secret code."

"A code?" She felt locked with him in this secret.

In her ear, he whispered, "All lovers have codes only they understand. Magic. To someone else, it means nothing. Maybe a trick. But for the two involved, it's a secret language just for them."

"Answer pray tell," Dawn said, remembering the trick with the dollar bill.

Eric nodded. "When Houdini died, he promised to send Bess a secret message from the grave, one only she would understand, so she would know he was still with her." Eric squeezed Dawn's sore hand but it did not hurt, not even a little. His slender fingers, soft and warm but a man's hand all the same, firm and gentle, entwined in her own (she rubbed his hand with her thumb). "To tell her that he loved her, always," Eric said. Something buzzed in her head and lit up like a firefly trapped in a jar. Eric slid his cheek across her face, then looked her in the eye. Some say that you could see Dawn's breath as if it were a cold day, the heat rising in her, coming out like steam. Something had been ignited in her, warmed her like a bonfire. His hand slipped from hers.

"That's impossible," she said, but their lips were almost touching now. "You can't send a message from the grave."

A grin and he pulled back slowly. Eric stood up, held out his hand, old-fashioned gentleman-style, and added, "Let's go to the Rosabelle, have some lunch."

"But you haven't seen all – "

"I've seen all I need to see."

And with that, she stood, his hand in hers.

At the Rosabelle Café, Dawn looked up at the wooden sign. It meant something more now, but she didn't ask Eric about his book dedications. She did not want to hear the answer. Maybe the buzzing in her head was not a harmless firefly but a fire alarm signaling danger, or maybe it was an alarm clock trying to wake her. Either way, she walked with him. With his hand in her own, Eric had been quiet the entire walk over. She thought he gave no clues, no hints. Could she live in that one glorious moment with his hot breath flickering eyes firm hands? Damn Rosabelle. Damn his list of good qualities that expanded infinitely. Would he eventually kiss her? Would he taste like the licorice gum that he chewed? Would she crumble in his hand like a brown leaf? The day was so damned sunny ... and she loved it.

They ordered lunch, sat in the regular spot by the window, and talked of nothing much until Dawn, the little tortured girl who no man had ever really loved, asked in hope – at least Bess, someone could experience something beautiful – "Did she ever get the code? Bess Houdini?"

"I thought you said it was impossible?" He pulled a piece of crust from his bread without looking at his sandwich. He watched her instead. It was indeed a sunny day, the type of day that might make children skip, play hopscotch, or jacks on the sidewalk. It was the type of day that would make lovers nuzzle under a maple tree, snuggle on a park bench, or talk of things that would lead to a kiss.

"I was just curious," Dawn said and shrugged, watched him take two potato chips and place them on his sandwich (he was still watching her though), and she pretended to be more interested in a plump grape on her plate. There was no brown spot in the center of this grape. It was ripe, juicy. She ate it. Sweet.

"No," Eric said matter-of-fact like reading from a dictionary. He took a few bites. "The code. She never got it. She gave up after waiting ten years." Eric mimicked Bess' quiet voice, "'Ten years is long enough to wait for any man,' she said." Eric watched Dawn closely. She was disappointed.

Ever since childhood, Eric had grappled with this story too. He knew there had to be a reason why she did not get the code. Now, after years of contemplating, thoughts tumbling like a Ferris Wheel, he understood. "The language of lovers can't be forced. It shows up in the oddest of places at the oddest of times but always at the right time."

His explanation did not matter; the cynic in Dawn returned. The icy woman, cold like funeral black, just as Eric had written in his poem, could return at any moment when fear and rejection were as obvious as a corpse on a slab. Not even for Bess, the wife of Houdini, could magic happen. "It's no surprise," Dawn said. "That's impossible. I hope she didn't believe it."

"Maybe she didn't wait long enough?" he added.

"You can't send a message from the grave, Eric."

"You don't think so?"

"No."

"You don't believe in the magic of love?"

"In love?" She almost laughed, stopped herself, felt bad.

"That's no way to think."

"You really do?" She shifted, uneasy, pulled a strip of crust from her bread just as he had done but she did not look at him. "I read one of your poems. My landlady had one of your books." She wished she hadn't said it.

"Which one?" Too happy.

"I don't remember." Too quick.

"Did you like it?" Eric was rarely unsure. His

poems, after all, were beloved. What Dawn thought made his heart pause ... a referee holding up a hand ... wait just a moment ... and ...

"A little sentimental." She wished she hadn't said that too. She hurt him again.

Did you know you may be her? Her! The ache in his stomach, now in his chest. "You don't like sentimental. You don't like romantic?" He wanted to say, "But I wrote these for – "

"You dedicate your books to a girl named Rosabelle," she said, both bold and afraid, but her tone that of a little dictaphone, the way she spoke when talking about unimportant things like work.

He smiled. "Yes. Rosabelle – "

"Who is she?" She acted concerned with her food, things more serious, but she had asked too quickly. He knew.

Eric took Dawn's hand and sang these words, "Rosabelle, sweet Rosabelle, I love you more than I can tell. Over me you cast a spell. I love you, my sweet Rosabelle." He smiled again, said softly, "It's a song."

A song. The flicker in their eyes returned in an arc between them. The last bit of ice in Dawn's cold heart melted. It was a river, flowing free. A little bead of sweat formed on Dawn's chest right between her breasts near her heart. It slid down her stomach, past her belly button, and landed – slipped beneath her neat skirt – just above the dark hair that resided between her legs in much the same way as rain had slid down Eric's body the night before.

That damaged girl, that lonely person, still in doubt even when rivers raged furiously within her, coming out in sweat in tears in secret juices flowing beneath her clothes, still had to ask, "But Rosabelle, for you, is she a real person?"

"Of course she's a real person." And he squeezed

that bandaged hand very gently.

That river flowing, raging, pushed into her eyes, cold. "You wrote that song for her?"

"I didn't write that song."

"Who did?"

"I don't know. It's an old song."

"Who's Rosabelle?"

"Dawn, I want to be with you."

Me? You.

"Join me tomorrow evening for a night of magic. The Grace Theatre. Eight o'clock," Eric said.

"Tomorrow evening?"

"You're not afraid of the moonlight are you?" he said with a smile and she shook her head.

There they sat. Secrets whispered between lovers ... in a café named Rosabelle with an orange leaf meeting a green along the city sidewalk and skipping and rolling and landing in a trickle of water from a hot spring and sticking staying dying rotting burning seeding growing ... over and over ... from dawn to dusk. Raging. Like a fire. In an arc. The flicker. All consuming. No more whispers. Only magic in moonlight.

Moonlight

The sky was slightly orange, dusk settling in. Eric tilted his fedora a little to the left, thought it made him look cool. The gray trilby with the black band had been his constant companion since finding it in a second-hand shop in London. The hat matched a pair of black-and-gray spectator shoes perfectly. Purchased at the same time, he had already resoled the shoes once, but kept them so polished that they looked brand new. With his pin-striped black vest over a black long-sleeved shirt, sleeves rolled up a quarter, he did not look like a man who belonged in our time. That is not to say he looked like a relic, long forgotten or abandoned, Eric was a gentleman dressed for an evening on the town, ready to open doors and pull out chairs for his lady, and he did these things not to be old-fashioned or impressive. He did it because it was the right thing to do, the nice thing to do. As dusk flowed seamlessly to evening, Eric checked for lint on his black slacks. When he walked out the front door of the Arlington, he too blended effortlessly with the blackness of the night ... but his heart was the moon.

Moonlight streamed through the open window reflecting a luminous halo around Dawn's head. An old chandelier clinked in the light breeze. The air felt warm, the sky clear. She stood in Mrs. Crumper's bedroom, wearing a canary-colored sundress, purple pumps, and a pearl necklace. Mrs. Crumper splayed a collection of jewelry on the dressing table. Each piece glinted against the warm light of the room. Dawn wished she had a ring to play with on her finger, something to do with her hands to release some nervous energy, but Mrs. Crumper was not looking for a ring.

"Ah, here it is!" Mrs. Crumper said, triumphant, holding up a pair of pearl earrings. "I never had much use for them. I know, I know, with the doilies, the tea, and the British accent, I should love these girlie things." She patted her gargoyle apron. "That's the thing about people. See a package, make an assumption, never know what's really inside until you open it."

"That was in *Forrest Gump*," Dawn said. She felt giddy, could not hide it.

"Wasn't he talking about life? And chocolates?"
Dawn shrugged.

"Well," said Mrs. Crumper, pulling back her hair, showing off her ruby earrings, "I prefer the fire myself."

"A bit much for me." Dawn took the pearl earrings, put them on. "How do they look?"

"I think a man might nibble those ears off later. I may be old but I know a date outfit when I see one."

"It's nothing like that. I'm just going out with a friend."

"I see. Well, love, just where are you and your *friend* going?"

"Magic show."

"Ah, magic."

Across town, very close though, footsteps could

lightly be heard, a magician walked alone ... moonlight guiding.

A single rose. It appeared out of nowhere. Dawn looked at it, right at her feet. It wasn't there before. She picked it up, looked around, wondering if anyone else had noticed. A small crowd waited outside the Grace Theatre; they paid her no attention. Before her eyes, another rose fell at her feet. She looked up, saw nothing, and reached down to pick up the flower. Dawn felt a little awkward, but had no time to look around for an explanation when another rose landed at her feet. Then several more. It rained roses. She peered upward, craned her neck to see. Others in the crowd were watching now too.

"There's a guy up there," Dawn heard a voice say. From the darkness, out stepped Eric, standing perilously on the edge of the marquee. Even in his all black attire, he stood out in the night sky, that heart of his, the moon lit behind him. "Hi, Dawn," he said, soft voice, seductive voice. Some in the crowd were surprised, others amused, all confused.

"Eric, come down from there," Dawn said in a whisper, afraid.

"Down there?" he asked. He stood too close to the edge; he looked like he was about to jump. The crowd gasped, wondering. Eric stretched out his arms like an acrobat balancing on a tight rope. He spun around, pretended to lose his balance only to catch himself just in time. The crowd got a little nervous, concerned. The whole time Eric wore a mischievous smile. "I can't come down there," he said.

"Stop it," Dawn said, worried.

"How many flowers do you have?"

"What?"

"Flowers. Count them, please."

She did as he asked. "Nine."

"Nine?"

"Yes. Come down now."

The crowd watched him walk back and forth as if pondering a predicament. "To have a dozen, you need three more."

"Eric, quit joking around and get down here."

"Three, right? Three is the magic number."

"Eric, this is not ... "

He sighed. "Are you sure you don't have the others? Look again." He stopped walking, motionless watching Dawn. The crowd, if they had been seated, would have been on the edge of their seats. What next? they wondered. Was this part of the show? Dawn looked down, two more flowers were at her feet. She stared at them for a moment before picking them up. Yes, part of the show, the crowd thought and clapped. Eric smiled. "One more," he said. Dawn looked down again but saw nothing. "Where could it be?" he asked and grabbed hold of a nearby scaffolding, leaping safely to the ground. He landed to applause, but not from Dawn. She stared at him suspiciously, but he saw the relief in her eyes. She was glad he was on solid ground. With a big grin, he said, "The last flower is hiding."

"Where?"

He took her purse, opened it, and pulled out the last flower. With a smile, he handed it to her.

"How'd you?"

"Magic."

The crowd clapped, except one. A young man. Dawn had seen him before but could not place him. "That's no big ta dig. They were in on that together. She had that in her purse the whole time."

Eric almost messed up and called him Travis but instead said, "I beg your pardon?" Eric took the flowers from Dawn, counted them. "Eleven. You miscounted." Everyone seemed confused, even Dawn. She had been sure it was right. Eric walked over to Travis, said very casually, "I believe you have something that belongs to my girl." He spun Travis around, and there in his back pocket, was the twelfth flower. The crowd laughed, applauded. Travis, enjoying the scene and being a pro, looked back at his behind. In comic fashion, Eric attempted to retrieve the rose, feeling a little uncomfortable about reaching into the boy's pocket. Even Dawn laughed and she wondered, how did he do it? Travis handed the rose to Eric. He took it, comically suspiciously, blew dust from it, rubbed it on his pants leg, and handed it to Dawn.

"Eric – " she started, but he put his hands up. He stuck out his arm for her to take and said, very simply, "Magic."

Flash. The camera flickered like a bright star as Dawn and Eric took a photo backstage with Floyd Donnelly, an old-school magician of about sixty with top-hat and tails. Just by looking at him, it was obvious he knew how to pull a rabbit out of a hat. Maybe not the best magician in the world, but he certainly fit the stereotype, along with his "lovely assistant," a woman half his age named Tina, who wore a beaded outfit that looked like a swimsuit with an ice-skating skirt. Her hair was as flaming red as her outfit. Houdini would have cringed at the entire scene. It all looked absurd.

"You're great with the sleight of hand," the magician said to Eric. "Terrific performance outside."

"Thanks." He winked at Dawn, who was still trying to figure out how he had done it. Before she could speak, Eric asked, "What's the story with the disappearing girl or whatever? Dawn wants to know."

"I do not."

"Oh, that's just part of the show," said Tina, handing

him a slip of paper to autograph. When they had taken the photograph, her hand had rested a bit too close to Eric's backside.

"There's truth to that story," the magician corrected. Dawn watched him closely. He believed it. "Her father even tried to kill him."

"It wasn't her father. It was her husband. Secret love affair," Tina said, gleefully happy with Eric's scribble on a piece of notebook paper. "They couldn't be together so they planned the whole disappearing thing and ran away together."

Eric pondered the story for a moment. "Could be. Makes sense. Lovers can't be apart. When you love someone, you want to be with them, will go to great lengths for it."

"Maybe," Dawn said but inside she was blushing at the way he had said "love" and looked right at her.

"That more logical?" Eric asked with a grin.

"Yes."

"She is much like Tina," said the magician. "She does not believe in magic."

"Nope," Eric replied. "Not a lick."

"It's not real," both women said at the same time.

And just then, nearly confirming Dawn's disbelief, Travis walked in, said hello to Eric and caught himself when he saw Dawn. He backed out slowly, pretending to be confused.

"Ah-ha!" Dawn pointed a finger at Eric, accusatory but in a friendly way.

He smiled, shrugged. "It was still magical, Dawn," he said in a whisper and took her hand.

A cardboard crescent moon hung from the stage, a backdrop lit to look like stars. Eric and Dawn sat dead center front row. The best seats in the house. From their vantage point, Dawn and Eric could see the wings of the stage clearly, the backstage area. Whatever trickery was part of the show, they should catch it, Dawn thought. The theater was very small, held only a few hundred or so. A large chandelier, a more ornate version of the one Mrs. Crumper had in her bedroom, hung above the audience. Heavy maroon drapery on the walls, the same ones that fanned out on either side of the stage and throughout the lobby.

After securing a pair of handcuffs to the magician's wrists behind his back, Tina curtsied to the crowd. Behind the magician was a large cabinet and a chair. "I want everyone to be assured that these handcuffs are indeed real. Might I have a volunteer from the audience to inspect?" the magician said, feigning distress over the tight cuffs. "You there, red shirt, second row, come up and have a look please."

A man walked on stage, enjoying every bit of it. He waved like a star and walked over to Tina. She took him by the arm, patted him gently on the chest, and smiled, never speaking to him. The audience member inspected the cuffs, nodded that they were real. Tina pulled over the chair and pointed for the man to sit down. She opened the cabinet's door, spun it around, and tapped each side to show any lack of trickery.

Eric leaned over to Dawn, whispered, "This trick is called metamorphosis. Houdini and Bess, this was their first trick together."

The magician stepped inside the cabinet. "A kiss in case this doesn't work out," he said to Tina. The audience chuckled, oohing and aahing at the passionate kiss. The door closed. Tina stepped out of the way. A small explosion, blinding the audience for a moment. Floyd, the old-school magician, was back on stage, hands free, bowing. But no Tina. He opened the box and there she stood. Tina stepped out and waved. Applause. The magician went over to the man from the audience. "Thank you for your help, but before you leave, I need those handcuffs back." Genuinely confused, the man looked around. Floyd reached into the man's front shirt pocket and removed the handcuffs that only moments before he had been wearing.

"He was in on it too," Dawn said to Eric.

"Maybe."

The audience did not care. They applauded and had fun. When it came time for the finale, the audience was thoroughly behind Floyd the Magician. Every trick, every moment, they clapped rapturously. Dawn found it all amusing, but kept trying to figure out every trick. Eric just watched, smiling, sharing a bucket of popcorn with Dawn.

"When you look around," the magician said, "you see a full house, but there is someone else here whom you cannot see."

"Oh good grief. Here it comes," Dawn quietly exclaimed. Eric giggled but shushed her.

"She's been trapped here a very long time. Many years ago a very unfortunate lady," continued the magician, "was called on stage to perform the disappearing act; however, when they opened the box, she was gone all right." Dramatic pause. "Permanently!" The crowded, awed by it all. "They were never, ever, able to make her reappear. Now she haunts this very theater." The audience waited impatiently, edge of their seats, waiting for what would be next. He joked, "Apparently, that magician never got to chapter twelve in the magician's handbook – how to make pretty girls reappear." The audience laughed. "Of course, a better chapter, for me really, might be how to make pretty girls appear out of thin air. Would have saved me a lot of trouble in high school."

"He thinks he's a comedian," Dawn said to Eric.

"Tina, will you come out, my dear? I need you for this one." Tina did not come on stage. "She's spooked by this trick. Spooked by a silly ghost story." Tina, from the wings of the stage, peered out and shook her head. "Oh, come on," he said. She was clearly not moving. He went to the wings, literally pulled her back on stage. She comically kicked and screamed.

"You know what happened during rehearsal! I saw her! The one who never returned. She's trapped ... *on the other side.*"

"Uh-huh." Floyd made a motion with his finger to show that Tina was nuts.

"I'm telling you. She told me she's going to use our disappearing box to return!" Tina appeared frightened. Dawn heard Eric giggle like a little boy. "She's going to replace *her* with *me ... on the other side.* Then I'll be trapped! Trapped!" Tina started to leave the stage but Floyd grabbed her. He held her close, and she kicked her legs in frustration.

"That's crazy. Just get in the box."

Afraid, Tina got inside. He closed the door, spun it, and opened it. Tina is gone! The audience applauded, looked around for any ghosts, saw none. A sad sigh of disappointment. He closed the door, spun it again, opened it, still no Tina. Floyd grinned sheepishly. He tried again. No Tina. Once more. No Tina.

"Excuse me," he said to the crowd. He went to the wings of the stage, whispered audibly backstage, "Bart, give me the handbook. I need to look something up. Hurry." He went back to the crowd, grinning like everything would be fine, just part of the show, nothing to really worry about. A book was handed to him. The title clearly read in large letters "The Magician's Handbook." He quickly flipped through it.

"Rabbits in hats, card tricks, ah, disappearing girls." The audience laughed and he read over the section.

"This is stupid," Dawn said, but Eric's shoulder

brushed against her and she liked that.

"Oh, yeah. I forgot the magic word!" said the magician, then exclaimed, "Abracadabra!" He opened the cabinet door and out came a woman in Victorian clothing. He gasped, as she pushed him aside, scowled at the crowd and ran offstage with a wicked laugh. The frantic magician ran after her; the crew, pretending to be worried, quickly closed the curtains.

"Well, that was just silly," Dawn said, as the audience erupted in applause and laughter.

"A little cornball, I agree." He looked Dawn in the eye as the magician, Tina, and the Victorian woman came out on stage to take a bow. "But fun though," he said. Dawn shrugged but smiled.

As they were about to leave, Dawn felt a tap on her shoulder. It was Will, who was ecstatic and asked, "Was that not awesome? Oh, man, yeah! I told you it was going to be sweet!"

"He was more comedian than magician," Dawn said and looked to Eric for support.

"Not everyone can be Houdini," Eric replied, took Dawn's hand, led her through the crowds, away from everyone and everything, and stepped with her, and only her, into the night.

As they walked along in the warm air of the moonlight, the starlight, the light from traffic lights and street lights and window lights, they looked like any couple coming home from a date. Anyone to pass them by, paid them no more attention than any other lovers on an evening stroll, but the thing is, when anyone got too close, close enough to almost brush against them, then they saw it, something that seemed like a trick, a magician's sleight of hand. There was that little golden light, people swore it was visible, that sparked between them.

"His tricks were transparent," Dawn said. "Maybe if they had switched the two girls immediately, it would have been interesting, but that much time passing, good grief, an entire football team had the time to get inside that box. Nothing to it."

"How'd he get out of those handcuffs, do you think, in the metamorphosis trick?"

"Obviously fakes."

"You know everything, don't you?" It was said friendly.

"The audience member was in on it ... just like a certain teenage boy helping a certain writer with his trick."

Eric put his hands up. "I have no clue what you're talking about."

"That man already had those handcuffs in his pocket when he went on stage, just like you and that boy with the flowers."

"Got it in your purse though. How'd I do that?"

She shrugged. "You also stole my watch the other day. Thief."

"Yeah," he said with a laugh. "But you still can't explain how he got out of the handcuffs."

"Fakes."

"Nope. They were real."

She stopped walking. "How do you know?"

"I just do."

"So how'd he do it then?"

"You can see through any trick, you tell me," Eric said.

"I don't know, but there is a trick to it." Annoyed, she walked on ahead of him.

"There is." He caught up to her and taunted. "Driving you batty. You don't know how he did it."

At her doorstep, Eric realized he had seen the apartment building before. The one that looked magnificent when he was on his way to repair his watch. The building with the brightly dressed lady, and the wiggling dog, and the Cosine Movers van – had that been Dawn's stuff he wondered. *She* lived on Rahner Street. A breeze blew through his hair, knocked his hat off. The wonder of it all...

He reached down to pick up his hat. "Come to my book signing tomorrow at Boots & Burdini," he said, adjusting the hat, then getting very close to her. "Free book."

"Are you going to tell me how he got out of those handcuffs?"

"I thought you were going to tell me." A little closer and she stepped back, bumping into the front door.

"I can figure it out."

"Haven't yet. How'd he escape, Dawn?" As he got even closer (was it possible?), their chests touching, breath mixing, she looked up at him.

"He had small hands. He slipped them out," she said.

Eric took her hand. "No." Quiet.

In a nervous voice, she said, "The screws on the cuffs were loose, the hinges or something, and he undid them."

Even quieter. "No." He put her hands on his shoulders, his hands on her waist, pushed her gently against the door, pinning her there. "How'd he escape?" His mouth, the little heart-shaped lips, were very close to her own.

"I don't know." Her voice was so quiet, it was barely audible, but Eric heard and he knew.

"The key," he said with a slight pause, "was in the kiss," and with that his lips almost touched hers. She looked into his eyes, as if looking into her own, because she saw this time, not just a flicker, but a reflection, something light something warm something of her own. Was it her face? Was it his? Yes, it reflected back – both, one.

With open mouth, and open eyes, and open souls, they kissed in the moonlight. Leaves rustling in the breeze.

Breezes

The brightness in the sky fell from the heavens quickly and lightly, but powerfully like a soft shower suddenly streaming into a dark desert at dawn. With the window open, Dawn looked at the perfect sun, perfect day, but it was the evening that had caused it, gave rise to this wonderful new light, brand new day, that had waited so long. Dry and empty like a desert. Cold and dark like a desert. Now wetted. Now warm. Now light. Powerfully there.

It was the end of the week, but for Dawn it was the beginning and a big step for her. Just before leaving her apartment, Dawn checked her hair and curtsied. A red sundress (that she had forgotten she owned) and lighthearted smile covered a bruised burned healing hand. The little dark spot was barely noticeable. She grabbed her purse and hurried to the pastry shop where she bought a box of chocolate iced doughnuts, a hot chocolate, and a black coffee. There was a slight breeze and it carried her forward, blowing the hem of her skirt and her hair.

Inside Boots & Burdini Book Shoppe, dressed in the same black slacks and black dress shirt from the night before but with a red handkerchief in his pocket, Eric signed his poetry with a left-sided grin, not a full one (because that one was reserved for his beloved). Each woman politely ogled, giddy and gay, and moved on, thinking about that smile. Next in line, a moment in his eyes – that weird spark – and dreamed over his words, to pretend to be the object of those words, or maybe just to be those words, his. From the corner of his eye, he saw Dawn. He wanted to laugh as she juggled both box and drink holder, steady as she made her way past the women in line. When she got to the table, he raised an eyebrow, tilted his fedora up a notch to get a better look at her. "Back of the line, miss," he said.

She smiled – the first time a smile brighter than his – and said, "I thought you could use something sweet."

The line waited.

"You look nice," she said, admitting.

"Thank you. So do you."

As they ate, Dawn passed out the books to each person in line. Eric signed, over and over, each time drawing a little airplane next to his signature. When the line came to an end, they stepped out into the daylight, the sunlight, the soft pat of their footsteps, the drumming sound of their hearts. They walked down Bathhouse Row, the center of the city, tourists all around, but they stood out like a dollop of glitter against black paper. Shimmering, in love.

The leaves blew gently around their feet. Eric picked one up (he held it gently, did not crush it, Dawn noticed), then he let it go and watched it sail away on a current. It hovered in the air, then flew down the sidewalk ... somewhere. Dawn turned to the old buildings, some were tinted with age, some restored so well they looked new. Would they ever die? Could they? Couldn't they be restored over and over again? Continually and perpetually and forever. Her thoughts, usually could not take much of that type of thought, but she wondered and said to him,

"We are looking at the same sights people a hundred years ago saw too." She nodded to the old buildings. "Maybe that's why I like old things."

"Maybe you like the old things because you've seen them before?"

"I don't think so."

"You don't believe in reincarnation?"

"Not really. Dead should be dead."

"Just like with magic, you're very pessimistic about death."

Dawn laughed. "Eric, I think most people are pessimistic about death."

He smiled. "S'pose so." He stopped walking and pondered her words. "Dead should be dead. Very eloquent."

She squeezed his hand. "I don't like talking about death, Eric."

"Death doesn't bother me. It's merely a change like gas to liquid to solid."

"Everyone I have ever known who has died, I don't care if they come back at all. Some I really prefer they didn't."

"What if it's someone you love? Your great love, for instance. You'd miss him, wouldn't you? Like Bess and Harry."

She quickly changed the subject, pointed at the bath houses. "Public bathing is bizarre. Isn't it strange that people did that?" she asked, holding firm to his hand, hoping the subject of death would die.

"Relaxing like a hot tub."

"Yeah. I guess so. Still weird."

Not wanting to push anymore, he changed the subject too. "If you like old-fashioned things like me, you should come see the hotel."

"Al Capone used to stay there."

"Will's info?"

"Yeah. He said John Dillinger and Billie Frechette spent Thanksgiving there once too."

"He knows his gangster trivia."

"He does indeed."

"Well, too bad the hotel is decked out in Halloween silliness right now."

"It's next Tuesday. Halloween."

"It's not a favorite holiday of mine. Houdini died on Halloween."

"You're a little obsessed with him."

"You want me to rattle off more facts?"

"No." She playfully bumped up against him.

"I'm going to anyway, because I like it and it's weird. Do you at least believe in synchronicity or meaningful coincidences?"

"Nope. And what does that have to do with Houdini?"

"Plenty. Did you know Houdini died at age fifty-two, and he was called 'King of Cards' for his ability to do card tricks – "

"– and fifty-two cards in a deck. Yes, I get it."

"Dying on Halloween, age 52, and Bess died in Needles, California, and Houdini was famous for doing a trick swallowing needles."

"He swallowed needles?"

"Just a trick."

"Yes, Eric, it's all very freaky, but it is *only* a coincidence."

"Life's magic, to us, seems like a mere trick but it's real. It's conscious. It's divine."

She stopped walking. "I'm in control of my life, Eric."

A warm smile. "Indeed you are. I never said otherwise."

"You're getting into the realm of destiny."

He nodded. "I'm staying on topic. Magic." He put his arm around her (she wanted to rest her head on his shoulder) and kept walking. After a few steps, he stopped to pick up an autumn maple leaf. He twirled it on its stem and asked, "Do you believe in signs?" The flicker of red-gold-then-orange. But still ...

She shook her head, watched the little leaf flick back and forth in his hand. She noticed, for the first time, that he had a scar on both wrists, not just the one she had noticed on the train. They were identical, but she did not ask him about them. "Why do you ask about signs?"

"Because I'm weird."

"I agree on that!" She laughed.

"Come on now, you have to believe in signs."

"Nope."

Eric rolled is eyes, fluttered the leaf in her face. "Nothing mystical or spiritual or religious?"

She shrugged and took the leaf.

"Always logical?" he asked.

She shrugged again, let the leaf fly away in the breeze as he had done earlier.

"What *do* you believe in?" With a sigh, he added as he walked on ahead of her, "Has there ever been anything, anything that is constant in your life, that you felt meant something, even if you don't know what, that keeps showing up like it's trying to tell you something?"

"There have been things, I guess, but they don't mean anything." She stood rooted to the ground; a breeze blew her hair.

Eric turned back to face her. "Maybe they do and you're not paying attention." He clapped his hands loudly. "Pay attention."

"You're a very strange man."

"Real magic, let's look at it like this. Say every

time something big happens in your life, you happen to see an apple."

"What?"

"Just pretend that is so. To you, apples start to mean something, more than just a delicious fruit. You see an apple, weird things happen later. Like a sign. Now, to everyone else, that is a coincidence, but to you it is not. You know it means something."

"Again, I would like to restate that you are a very strange man."

"Do you understand, though? Real magic is personal. It's relative." Grinning, Eric held her at arm's length by putting his hands on her shoulders. "As a little girl you had a pet that you liked."

"What?"

"Real magic. I'm going to tell you what it was. There's no way I could know it."

"Oh brother. Are you serious?"

"Write it down on a sheet of paper."

Dawn took a pen and notepad from her purse and did as he asked. He instructed her to crumble the paper and throw it in the nearby garbage can. Eric rolled up his sleeve, held his hands out to show no trickery, and proceeded to take a handful of dirt. He then rubbed the dirt over his arm. Magically, the word "dog" appeared on his arm.

"I never had a dog."

"You have to admit it's pretty cool how I got that word to appear on my arm though."

She rolled her eyes and gently punched him in the arm. He pretended to topple over. She gave him a tissue and he wiped the dirt off his arm. The word stayed. "Your magic," she said, "might be worse than the guy we saw last night."

"What makes you think I'm finished with the trick?

Just keep watching. My magic is stupendous."

"Is it?"

"Stupendous!" he said with arms held wide. "Just wait."

They walked on a little farther and Dawn listened to the soft click of his shoes. She looked down at his feet. He wasn't wearing the spectator shoes from the night before but the same shoes from the train, the ones he had worn all week. Both sets gleamed. "You wear shiny shoes."

"I keep them polished."

"That says something about you."

"What, do you think?"

"I don't know exactly." She pondered for a moment. "Look at you," she said, and he stopped walking. "Your hair is this, I don't know, kinda wild untamed sort of thing that you keep tucked under a hat, but even so it always sort of dangles out the sides, all unkempt."

"Are you saying I need to comb my hair?" he said, taking off his hat and running his fingers through his brown locks.

"And you always wear black –"

"I'm a poet."

"That's cliché."

"You like kites?" he asked.

"Are you listening to me?"

He nodded, put his hat back on.

"Your shoes, when I first saw you, they didn't go with the rest of your clothes."

"Go with the hat." He flicked the brim once.

"There's a tear in the hat."

"Is there?" He took off the hat again, looked at the small tear in the brim, the type of split you might see in the ear of a dog who had one too many fights and lost one. He shrugged again.

"That's just it. Your shoes being shiny. It says

something about you. That you're not exactly who you appear to be."

"Who am I then?" He adjusted the hat on his head, angled it slightly so it was lower on one side, and sat down near a public drinking fountain that spewed mineral water from the local hot springs. Eric put his hand in the warm water, caught some, and took a sip.

Dawn sat next to him. "When I first saw you, I thought you were bohemian, maybe a backpacker or something, that you were quiet and mysterious, but you're not."

"I am too mysterious. Look at me here brooding and pondering the meaning of life," he said, squinting his eyes, crossing his legs, and stroking his chin. "I need a goatee. That'd make me more poetic."

"It's the shiny shoes. They give you away."

He clicked his shoes together. "Shiny shoes are classy. There's nothing like a good pair of refined dress shoes."

"Smooth and debonair, eh?"

"I'm not very smooth, but I am quite debonair." He winked.

"I like it."

"I know ... "

She looked away. "The shoes."

"Yeah? But do you like kites?"

"Why?"

"Let's fly one. There's a nice breeze."

"That's kind of cliché too."

"Are you so concerned with clichés? You know why they are clichés, Dawn? Because they work. They're good. Happens one time, good, again, good, keeps happening because of it. Becomes a cliché. Cliché is good." He put his hand under the fountain again and flicked the water onto her face. She gently shoved him and wiped her face. "Do you know the artist Efram Corbet?" he asked and

Dawn nodded. "He told me that once, about clichés."

"He paints portraits of sensuous women."

"He paints romantic scenes." A little drop of the hot water was still on Dawn's cheek. Eric rubbed it into her skin. "Just like I write – "

"I don't know where to buy a kite," she interrupted. His finger rubbing into her skin –

making little circles – "There's a hobby store near a watch repair shop. You might have seen it," he said.

"Okay." Still touching –

"It's not far from your apartment." Not far from her lips –

– Dawn touched his hand, held his fingers. "We can walk it then."

"You had a little drop of water on your face," he said, entwining his fingers in hers.

She wanted to kiss his fingertips but did not. Were his fingertips as soft as his mouth? They felt as soft. Did they taste the same? "Licorice," she said quietly aloud, re-membering last night's kiss. Sweet mint.

"What's that?" Eric asked, removing his fingers from her grip and running it through her hair.

"Nothing," she said and they locked eyes. She saw that familiar bright glow. Red-gold-then-orange. Hot in the center, the core, a layer of richness, strong, then warm and gentle on the edges, so gentle you could touch it, feel it like the outer petals of a tiger lily (open at dawn, closing by dusk). It would not burn. It would not hurt her. "You're not mysterious at all. You're ... you're ... " – she shrugged a little – " ... vulnerable."

Shocked. "Vulnerable?" Never in his life had he heard such a thing. For a moment he thought about it and let his fingers untangle from her hair.

Dawn tried to explain. "You're like a ... I don't know ... you have this veneer, that you can't be hurt, things bounce off you, but your inside is tender and – ”

"I want to fly a kite." He knew some day a girl would see past his flickering eyes to the soft inside, the soft dough still rising consuming him slowly. Inside, past the women who broke out in sweats when he walked past, beyond the magazine-voted handsome writer, far away from the cool guy in tattered hat and shiny shoes, was the boy unraveling a thread from a grandma-made quilt. "It's a nice day to fly a kite," he said, voice soft like a breeze.

"Let's fly a kite then," she said, kicked his shiny shoes playfully, left a little scuff.

"You're going to polish those," he said and ruffled her hair.

She gently shoved him – he tugged her hair – like two children who want to say "I like you" but don't know how. Of course Eric did know – told the vulnerable boy to stop unraveling the quilt – and he played along. Dawn pinched his arm and he pinched back. "Ouch," she said and reached out for a gentle slap, but he ducked and he ran. After him, she went because she was suppose to and she knew it and they went, row after row of old buildings, a park, and a cemetery. Off they went in search of a kite to fly, to mix with the puffy white clouds, near heaven, near perfection because it was cliché and cliché was something that happened over and over because it was good. Their beating hearts faster as they ran until Eric stopped and called a truce, hands up, defeated. They slowed and walked; she leaned against him, feigning a stumble, felt his breath rising, his heart pounding – was it just from running?

"I thought you were pretty," he said when they had calmed, a quiet stroll, and found what they were looking for. She stopped and looked up at him. What had he just said? "That's what I thought when I first saw you. That you were pretty. My first impression. I still do."

That's what she wanted to hear, needed to hear, and the last vestiges of any cruel word from her mother who was suppose to have been born a boy, a mean joke from a high school boy who had licorice breath but he was the wrong boy, hateful actions of a grown man who locked train cars with padlocks, or lack of love from a father in jail and a grandfather in hell, it all left her in one flick, quick, like a flip of a page, a snap of a finger, not even leaving a fragment of thought.

Somewhere in Altus the hinges on a little caboose rusted through, fell off, leaving the pages of lost notebooks and journals, the photos of boys who did not love back, to fly into the air, drop to the ground, and land in the mud to be buried and gone.

Eric squeezed her little hand, looked at it, the bruise near gone, and kissed it. The breeze blew around them, stirred up autumn leaves, and nudged them forward. Two tumbled together, in much the same way as Eric and Dawn, giddy and free, following the current. Tumbling and falling tumbling and falling. Giddy and free. Flying like birds. One landed and stopped on a small mound of earth, a tree before it without leaves, standing like a headstone. The other waited nearby.

Flight

It is a wonderful thing to be in love. The most wonderful of them all. Few people wish to admit it, thinking it
childish romantics, society treating romantic love like
fool's gold, but love and all its glory is the point the origin
the everything of anything. Without it, nothing. Eric knew
it, and even though he was becoming increasingly frus-
trated trying to put together a ten-dollar kite made of plastic
and flimsy board, he appreciated the wonder of his heart on
this perfect day – sun gleaming a blue sky and making re-
flections on the swingset slide, the scarcity of people in the
park as if Dawn and Eric had their own private playground,
a tire swing lolling gently as if floating on a calm lake, the
still-green grass with a grasshopper on a fallen golden leaf
(gently chewing), and of course Dawn with hair blown by
the subtle breeze (although she was laughing at Eric for his
ineptitude at kite-making). They were seated on the soft
grass. Both barefoot.

"Ugh!" Eric said, throwing up his hands and letting
the kite pieces fall to the ground. "This shouldn't be this
complicated."

"Just give it to me," Dawn said, picking up the pieces.

"I'm not mechanically inclined. I'm a writer. What do you expect?" Eric rested on his back, hands behind his head, and stared at the sky. Birds soared and chirped. Dawn fitted the slats together and the kite started to take shape. Eric looked over at her. "You're very good at that. You know where things go, things fit." He kicked her gently. "So organized."

"I like things that go together being together."

"As it should be."

"You think you're so smart?" she said without being able to come up with any other response.

"You know, Miss Dawn Corner, I was thinking, historians by nature hold on to the past, preserve it. Why not let those crusty papers disintegrate? Why care about old-fashioned things at all? Those moments are over, gone, if you really believe dead should be dead, the end. *The end.* Why save it?"

She stopped working on the kite for a moment. "Maybe, Eric, I just don't know. Some people should stay dead, don't you think? The wicked ones? But everyone, I guess not, but I just can't believe in that. It's not logical, living again."

"And dying is logical?"

"What's the point in living again?"

"Plenty of reasons. To have fun. To experience. To learn," he said with a shrug, sitting up on his arms. "To get something right you messed up last time."

She finished working the tabs into each slot. With a quick glance, she asked, "Do you think you messed something up the last time? Is that why you think like that?"

"Maybe. For all I know I'm messing something up right now."

She shook the kite as a joke. "You didn't do so good with this."

Laying back down, he nodded. "And I'll never learn a thing with you doing it for me. I'm okay with that."

She attached one last piece to finish the kite. "Ta da!" she exclaimed. Just then, with the kite held high in her arms, a yellow canary landed atop it, just like the one who had been on her windowsill, just like the one she had let fly away as a girl. Dawn dropped the kite, and the bird flew away.

"That was weird. I had a canary as a little girl."

"Logic," Eric said.

"What?"

"You said it's not logical to live again. What are the chances that a bird like the one you had as a child would land on your kite after we had been talking about childhood pets earlier? That doesn't seem logical but it happened. Explain that."

"Coincidence."

"A meaningful coincidence ... maybe a sign?" he asked simply and rolled up his sleeve. Written in ink, above "dog," was the word "canary." He picked up the kite and stood. "Magic," he said running away, preparing to fly the kite.

Dawn sat for a minute, a warm flush in her chest, not fear ... was it love? Was it joy? Could this be real? No. It was a coincidence. "Are you some kind of warlock?" she said, joking, running after him.

"See, now, that, that's illogical." He turned to face her, nearly running backwards, unraveling the string on the kite as he went. "Did I not tell you that my magic was stupendous? You have no faith in my abilities!" A gust of wind picked up the kite and it sailed, twirled on its plastic wings, flimsy cardboard holding it together with the sheer act of the miraculous, and they both watched it fly. The truth was, however, that Eric was just as amazed at the little canary as Dawn had been. When he had written "canary" earlier it had been merely the first word that had come to his mind. It had seemed absurd so he had quickly changed it to "dog." He knew better to doubt his gut feeling again and unleashed a little more kite string. It went higher, and Dawn rushed over, yelling, "Don't let it get away!"

"Don't worry," Eric reassured. "I've got a good grip on it." Dawn stared at the kite, as Eric let loose even more string; it went farther, slowly becoming a speck, but they could still see it, the orange kite with a white ghost (made for Halloween) blending with the background blue sky. Eric held the string tight; Dawn put her hand over his. No matter how far the kite flew, how far away, the string held it to the ground – the kite Dawn fashioned, the one Eric reigned in with a firm yet gentle grip. From the corner of her eye, Dawn saw Eric, the real man closer and clearer than she ever had (not just vulnerable), and she didn't need to know how he did it, the little act of magic, and he would never tell her, because it was not the kind of magic that could be explained, only witnessed between lovers, the secret language of two. In a nearby tree, the canary sang.

"That's real freedom," said a deep voice behind them. They both turned to see a handsome man in his thirties, moustache and goatee, tattered brown fedora (Eric instantly loved it), and bomber jacket with a patch that said "39." In his pocket was a harmonica. He held out his hand. "Heathcliff Brown." His voice was slow and cool. They both shook his hand; Eric kept one hand firm on the kite. "For fun, I barnstorm in Colbert's Field a couple miles away," he said, handing them a flyer. "I take people for flights, ten bucks, up where the kites and canaries fly." Heathcliff looked to the sky. Their kite was nearly invisible. "You want to experience the real thing?"

"Not really," Dawn said.

"You do any skydiving?" Eric asked.

"Eleven bucks." His smile was friendly, and Eric

thought he resembled the writer Ryan Ingram, old-fashioned with a disdain for computers.

"Is that your plane I've seen flying around town?"

"Most likely."

"You want to jump out of a plane?" Eric asked Dawn.

"Of course not!" she said, although she did not have to say it, because the look in her eyes was plenty.

"You don't want to jump out of a plane?" Eric asked her again, knowing she did not.

"No thank you."

"I do."

"What do you mean, you do?"

Eric handed the reigns of the kite to Dawn and pulled the man aside. In a weird moment, instinct intuition, whatever deep knowing we all possess, Dawn saw it. The kite was too high; it tugged at her hand. It wanted to break free. On the ground, the green grass, so soft and perfect between her toes. Not now, she thought. They had just sat together, happy and free. She could hear Eric's words, what he wanted to do. Was that white cloud in the distance, the one so near to their kite, becoming black?

"Don't do it, Eric. Please," she said, whispering, fearing. That weird strange magical moment of knowing – it hit her like a slap of thunder if thunder were no longer a sound but a beastly object with force and matter, solid and real, and not of anything intangible or unseen. And she looked at the grass, let the kite go. The string fell to the ground, the spool unraveled rapidly, tumbling, as if trying to run after the lost kite. It went far out of reach. Dawn saw it, not the kite, or the string, but something ... For the first time, the thought of Eric did not warm her, it froze her to that spot, frigid blow, snapping the cheap string of the kite with a hard gust. She panicked and cried out for Eric.

"Dawn, let it go!" Eric called back, thinking she

was screaming about the kite. "It's not important." But
Dawn knew that. The kite was long gone. She was not
crying for it, but for Eric. While Dawn did not understand
completely, she understood dread and fear. "Don't jump,"
she said, but Eric did not listen. His mind was set, and
when his mind was set on something, he did not turn back.
He would jump, and he would do it to make Dawn believe
in magic. See, this is the way things are, and always will
be. Some of us are magicians, knowing all the tricks, as
Eric has and always will. Just like the great Houdini, and
just as he told Dawn, his magic ... stupendous. Others, the
watchers, the learners, the bewildered and confused will
buy a ticket and take a chance until they learn how the trick
is done and become stupendous too. Dawn watched Eric
laugh with the barnstormer, as if he knew what was going
to happen, as if he wanted it to happen. She did not. They
had spent this lovely week in happiness, and he was choos-
ing to end ... There was (and never will be for any soul) a
fear as great as the one she felt at that moment. I love you
(but she did not speak it out loud). The canary still sang;
she looked for it. There, in the apple tree, with blossoms
and ripe fruit, it danced with its wings and flew away.

Dance

There is a common misconception, perpetuated by self-help gurus, that love is an action. If this were so, then it would cease to exist. While the actions of Dawn and Eric would surely come to an end, the love they shared would remain, floating and alive in space in time.

"I don't want you to do it," Dawn said as Eric handed her a slice of "bread of the dead," a sweet roll flavored with anise. All around them dusk had settled in, the autumn trees like skeletons, and people walked around the cemetery celebrating the Mexican holiday of Dia de los Muertos, a festival of the dearly departed. Sitting on the ground, Eric was happily eating the bread and watching people in skeleton face masks perform dances. The music was joyous; this is not a holiday of mourning. Dawn picked up a candle from one of the many altars that were on various graves. The one they sat next to was for an elderly couple. Their family had adorned the side-by-side head-stones with flowers, family photos, and rose petals. "Are you listening to me?" Dawn asked, reading a note a child had left near the grave.

"Yes," Eric replied, mouth full. "I've sky-dived plenty of times. There's nothing to worry about." They had been arguing about it all afternoon, through lunch, through dessert, and now as they sat watching the festivities.

"But you're doing it in handcuffs!"

A few people turned around to look at them. Eric kissed her forehead. "It's going to be fine. All part of the show." He took her face in his hands. "There's always a trick to it, remember?" he added and Dawn shrugged. "Now, relax and have some fun. This is our day, our night. Let's not spoil it."

She snatched the last of the bread, ate it, and took a sip of Coke. "I thought the Day of the Dead was after Halloween?"

"It is but some places have festivals before. It's nice to celebrate the lives of those who have passed on, to make it happy, not sad." Eric had been sitting cross-legged on the ground, and he stretched his legs out, then stood up. "Let's buy a candle for Bess and Harry."

They walked over to a small stand that sold everything from nesting dolls to skull rings. Dawn looked at one of the colorful Mexican shirts, while Eric picked out a bright red candle. The stand attendant gave Eric a box of matches. "Let's light it together," Eric said, taking Dawn's hand. They walked past another stand with children getting their faces painted with the traditional skeleton masks. "You want to do that?" Eric joked. She shook her head. They found a spot near a large maple tree. Eric cleared the area of dried leaves, and they both got down on their knees. "For Bess and Harry," Eric said and Dawn repeated. "And for us," Eric said, that flicker in his eyes. He handed the candle to Dawn, and she held it still as Eric lit the wick, that same flicker before his face, between them. The little blaze streamed upward, sending a tiny dancing swirl into the air.

A child twirled past them, whispered, "There are ghosts in the night. They dance and speak without fright. This is their night." It was a childish playful taunt, meant to sound mystical and a little spooky in a youthful way, but Eric had a halo around him that danced around the edges of his face. It glowed orange. But that flicker was burning red, brighter than the candle; his eyes blended with the flame as if he were fire itself. While Dawn's heart pumped the same fire, she could not help but notice the way Eric appeared to be fading, shadowy haze around him. He looked like a ghost.

Eric bought two tickets, handed one to Dawn. The doors of the MJ Music Box were heavy red doors that looked like velvet, varnished and tarnished to match the flash and color of the wailing music inside. People were swinging and dancing and laughing and having the gayest of times. Up front on stage, a man with long dark hair, faded jeans and Fender T-shirt, was loudly strumming a guitar and singing in a deep soul voice. He certainly did not look like the type of person to have that voice. It caught Dawn off guard like hearing Jonny Lang sing for the first time. Eddie Field looked like he should be the leader of a simple rock band, but his style was a mixture of classic rock and big band and swing and blues and soul and every-thing anything he could throw into the pot. On stage, his stew bubbled over. It was musical gumbo.

To the side of the stage a little boy with red hair bopped along to the beat, far too young to be in the club, but he stood out of the way and no one seemed to mind as he drank a Shirley Temple and scooted around like a young James Brown. Everyone twirled and swirled about the dance floor. Some were swing dancing – a man lifted a woman high in the air and spun her around. Some were bouncing with their hands in the air. Two men gyrated seductively against one another. Mrs. Crumper was in a far corner doing something that resembled the jitterbug – all alone, but she was having the best time of all.

The joint was one big party, no sadness, all laughter. In her entire life Dawn had never seen so many smiling faces. The bar was packed; a man gave Dawn a little wink, and Eric pulled her close. Before Eric could order drinks, Will came over, all smiles, with Floyd's lovely assistant Tina. "This rocks!" he said. "It's too cool!"

"I'm going to admit," Eric said, "that this is indeed cool."

They all saddled up to the bar, ordered a few drinks and watched the band. Whispering in Eric's ear, Will said, "Notice Tina has red hair. Red! Just like Sledge said. I'd meet a red-haired girl. Wild."

Eric smiled. "Mystical janitor."

The music got a little softer; Eddie put his hand up letting the band know he had something to say. "Hot Springs, are you hep to the jive?" he asked. The crowd wailed, "Yas, yas!" Sledge, who had been singing backup, slid to the front of the stage ala Jackie Wilson and let loose a soulful croon, complementing the tune perfectly. The beat jumped back up.

"Musical janitor," Will said.

Eric nodded in time with the music. "Out of sight." He put his drink down, took Dawn's drink and put it on the bar too. "Let's dance."

"You dance?" Dawn asked.

"What, you think poets can't dance?"

"Is your dancing stupendous?"

"Just like my magic."

"I can't dance."

"Sure you can. Everyone can dance." He took her hand and twirled her next to him. She giggled when he nuzzled her neck. He circled her and tickled her sides.

Dawn tried to get away but he was too fast and pulled her onto the dance floor. Quickly, he dipped her backwards. When he pulled her back up, Eddie pleaded with someone to come up and jam too. "You promised, man," Eddie said. For a moment the man hesitated, while Dawn and Eric kept dancing. A little more pleading, the crowd in on it too. Dawn and Eric looked around; there was the barnstormer leaning against the wall, cool-like. In a few moments, the sound of a harmonica, and Heathcliff was on stage joining in the music fracas.

"Musical pilot. Dig that," Eric said, twirling Dawn. "One cool cat. Hey, that rhymes."

"Poet."

"Don't I know it!"

Mrs. Crumper twirled over. "Might I cut in?" She winked at Dawn, whispered, "Guess you made it to that book signing?" Dawn introduced, "This is my landlady." Eric bowed and took Mrs. Crumper's hand. Dawn watched them dance for a moment before Mrs. Crumper spun herself silly. The landlady giggled, gave Eric a playful little pinch on the behind, and said, "You really know how to move those buns, dear." Dawn laughed. Before Mrs. Crumper headed to the bar, she whispered in Dawn's ear, "Ooh la la! I told you his words were magic, and he's a good little dancer to boot."

"She pinched me!" Eric said, rubbing his behind. Dawn couldn't stop laughing. "Oh, you think this is funny?" Eric grabbed Dawn again and spun her a few times, making her dizzy.

"Eric, too much!" she said but she was laughing, really laughing, and she did not care if anyone heard or anyone saw that everything was out open alive ... even her, the once-tortured girl who was locked tightly in the arms of a poet who wrote love verses and it no longer mattered who Rosabelle might be because his eyes, she knew this without doubt, were flickering red-gold-then-orange for her.

A little gust of wind from all the bodies in motion around them flipped Eric's hat to the ground. He picked it up and put it on Dawn's head. Seductively, Eric walked around her, sizing her up for a moment, then he grabbed her around the waist and pulled her close. That girl, who had never danced before, picked up the steps, as if she had been practicing her whole life for this moment. Cheek to cheek, as if they were about to do the tango, Eric said, "Dance with me."

"We are dancing." Cheeks flushed.

Eric shook his head, because Eric knew that love was not an action, but a simple unending dance with a rise and flow crescendos and waltzes quiet moments blazing guitars and static and noise and pat-pat patty-pat of shoes and strumming humming drumming fumbling stumbling swing divining shimmering symbols and Bess and Harry and Harmony and Everett and Grandma and Grandpa and melody and heat and soul and buttermilk and Rosabelle, all a swirl, all a go, never to cease, never to die. All senses ... always alive.

$\mathcal{S}$enses

The hotel was quiet. The only thing Dawn could hear, and she was sure Eric could hear it too, was the thump-thump of her heart and the shallow panting of her breath. When they had stepped inside the lobby, Dawn ignored the old-fashioned feel of the hotel. Normally, it would have charmed her, but she could only see a long hallway ahead of her. Golden elevators, the ding as they opened, and knew in a matter of seconds she would be rising up in the elevator with Eric on the way to his room. Her palms were sweating and she rubbed them on her dress. A couple sat in the bar, snuggled close, as a jazz band played the seductive *Passion Flower*, very different from the raucous atmosphere of the MJ Music Box. At the elevator, Eric took her hand and they needed no words. Speaking in that silent language of love, internal and knowing, the same way sunlight speaks to plants, they were entwined, toward a consummation that would engulf them like the sun.

Dawn glanced up at him in little quick flashes as they stepped into the elevator. For a man who Dawn saw as the all-consuming flame, he was calm, a fire burning quietly in the distance. It bothered no one, gave no indication, that it was burning, raging, lapping ... until you looked at its core ... his eyes, red hot. Staring now, Dawn could not turn away, mesmerized, and she followed him out of the elevator to room 1926.

Eric opened the door, this time using his key. His mind was not on that kind of magic. He held the door open, like a gentleman, and let Dawn step inside. Being in tune as he usually was, he motioned for her to take a seat on the sofa, knowing she was afraid, and walked over to the bar. Dawn saw his blanket slung over the couch. She picked it up and sat down with it, secretly sniffed it.

"My grandmother made it for me," he said. "You see that blue patch in the center? That's from my baby blanket, the one I was carried home from the hospital in."

"Ah," Dawn said with a teasing grin, "that's so cute. Is it your blankey?"

"It's a good blanket." Eric rummaged around at the bar.

She fingered the little blue patch, looked closely at all the swatches of material, then touched the one of the inkwell and quill – the first one she had seen when he let her borrow the blanket on the train.

Eric noticed her looking at it. "That's the last one my grandmother made. Just before I went off to college. At first, I thought I was going to delay entry into school, because I didn't want to leave her. I think she knew, though. She died just before fall semester, quietly in her sleep one night."

"You miss her. I can tell. I was never close to anyone in my family." Dawn held the blanket close and looked out the window at the night sky. Stars. So many. A pitch black night but lit with so many brightly twinkling stars. There was something so peaceful about it, and Dawn became immersed in the look of the sky and the feel of his blanket. She turned to look at him when he accidentally clinked two glasses together. He brought them to the coffee table, then went to his trunk that was open on the floor. When he turned around, he had a sneaky look on his face. "You like old-fashioned things?" he asked. "Want to try something a little adventurous?"

With a green bottle of liquor in his hand, he sat down next to Dawn. She took the bottle from him. "Absinthe? That stuff will make you crazy."

"I'm already crazy."

"Now we know why."

He opened the bottle and she seemed unsure. "It's diluted with water and sugar. Just don't drink too much," Eric said, making the drink. The green liquid turned cloudy for a second as the water and sugar mixed. Eric handed Dawn a glass. With a clink of glasses, they took a sip.

"Tastes like licorice," she said and he nodded, leaned back on the sofa. Dawn kept her eyes on the drink, swirled it around a little. "Let's see, Eric Pilot, you drink absinthe, you're a writer, you hang out in cafes ..." He nodded in agreement to all. "You take trains across country, like old-fashioned hotels. Magic too. Do you also like Paris in the springtime?"

"Yup."

"Or maybe Amsterdam?"

"I love Amsterdam. Am I a cliché?" he asked.

She leaned back; he put his arm around her. "You belong in a different time," she said. Their eyes locked and they belonged nowhere but right there right then. They let the alcohol relax them, calm any hidden fears and doubts, and Eric revealed a secret to her (but not vulnerable). "I sense I don't belong anywhere."

"That's not true."

He smiled.

"Where would you be?" she asked. "In a 1920s café in Paris discussing existentialism?"

"Maybe, but not discussing existentialism. Those people are such downers. Cold and dead inside. Life has meaning." He gave her a hard stare.

She shrugged, but the alcohol was making her giddy. "Up on stage like Houdini then?"

He looked into her eyes and shrugged. While her eyes, with the more she drank, were starting to get a little unfocused, her heart he knew was quite focused and steady in its beat and rhythm and knew exactly what it wanted and needed. Eric said, "I just feel ... do you ever feel alone? Like there's someone out there who's suppose to be with you, that you've always known, that belongs in your life no matter where or when you live, and if you find that person then ... then you'll belong ... you belong to them, with them ... like maybe you've been looking for them your whole life and that's all that matters?"

She nodded, drunkenly, and patted his chest. "You really really really believe that stuff you write, don't you?"

"I believe some people belong together." He scooted closer, took both drinks, and placed them on the coffee table. Very closely, he pulled her next to him.

Seduced, Dawn asked, "Do you think we belong to-gether?"

He nodded and leaned her back on the sofa. Gentle kisses on her neck, and her voice only a breath. "Eric, you're the only one ... " she said but his full weight was upon her and she made no move to stop him.

The moon was the only light. The only sounds, just as when they had entered the hotel, heartbeats and breath. Alone in his bed, their bed. The kissing continued beyond her neck, her mouth, her breasts, her navel. Beyond, in her mind and his, mere flesh. The kisses went somewhere so deep it felt unhuman. The moment was so heady, Dawn did not know what she liked most. The heat of his breath? The feel of his tongue? The five o'clock shadow that had gone way past five? Maybe the gentle way the tip of his nose barely touched her skin? No, she realized, in a lucid moment, it was none of those things. It was the way his hands held her legs apart. The way he had opened her legs only moments before, kept her there with those hands, pushing her down, keeping her open to him. His hands. On her. Her. Her! One thumb playing with her most tender skin, the other caressing her thigh. But on her. Her. Her! This handsome man was making love to her. And his thoughts were only on Her! And she cried, not merely because it felt good. He loved her. And he continued to kiss her there, not merely because he enjoyed it. He loved her. She ran her fingers through his hair, pulled him closer and deeper and let him inside, not merely because he loved her. She loved him. And, Eric felt her fingernails scratch the back of his neck and loved it, not merely because they were her fingers. She loved him. And that, as has been known from the past the now and forever, was the point. When face to face, their lips touched, a wave of heat from their mouths and both their eyes were fire. Not a flicker. Not a red-gold-then-orange, but an intense flame like a burst from the sun. A solar flare. All consuming. Even in all that rage, Eric's body slowed and with a very gentle push he entered her, not just her body, but her very soul, the place he belonged. In that crazy moment of passion, she said to him in a cry that must have surely been heard throughout the city because on that night, the evening sky peppered with lust, it would be claimed years later that the moon suddenly glowed red and women wept and felt their bodies grow moist, children awoke in the night covered in tears, and even the most pious of men dropped to their knees begging forgiveness at the lascivious thoughts in their minds – all this just at the sight of the moon, because true love can change the moon and the stars and the very night sky and the darkness will flow with the blood of lust, and Dawn yelled one thing, the most meaningful of all things, she said simply but with the living fervor of green, "You belong with me!" Alive. Every sense in the body agreeing, their pale skin pleasured in red.

There was that moon looking back at them from the window, matching the fire on their skin, the blood that ran in trickle between her legs, and Eric looked into those ruby-colored eyes (his reflecting the same), eyes now like a drop of red on white paper, and said, "Always." The sheets tangled, the floor creaked, and tears rolled from his eyes.

A couple in the room next door stopped having sex, because that is all they were doing, having sex, not making love like Eric and Dawn, and they listened, wished, and felt lonely. Downstairs in the lobby, a pen rolled off the front desk. Did the building just shake? wondered the few guests in the lobby. Was it an earthquake? A truck rumbling past? The saxophonist in the band wailed; he could feel it so powerfully, the note that escaped caught the attention of those walking past on the street, who were already stupefied by the blood red moon and the swaying – was that what was going on? – of the hotel walls and the one window way up top that was steamed over (the only one).

A candle burning under a maple tree for Bess and Harry blew out. The remaining leaves on the Hot Springs trees fluttered but there was no real wind now. No clouds. Only stars. And that bloody moon. What caused the branches to sway without a breeze? What caused steam to rise from chimneys without a fire and unboiling tea kettles to whistle? What caused it but love. Real genuine honest love. A love that held its grip, never dying, unable to shake. The residents in that town never did shake it, and will tell the story of the blood red moon, the way it enticed and flickered (was it first red-then-gold-then-orange?), gathering and holding everyone so still and so shocked and so filled with desire. That city never recovered, and if you walk those streets today, you will see lovers hand in hand, looking for that moon, that flicker in one another like candle light, locked in tender embraces.

Candles

There was a fog outside. The moon was white, back to its natural hue. They could see it through the window. They paid it no attention though; candles were lit throughout the bedroom, little flickers of light. The swirls of candle smoke were blown by the gentle hum of a fan. Eric's heart was beating slowly now, his breath shallow, but his eyes were open and he was looking at the little piece of Dawn's hair that usually stuck out slightly to the side. That piece of hair that she had always tried in vain to get to stay down was completely relaxed, blended with the rest of the strands as if it had never in its entire life been an untamable nuisance.

Her heart was beating rapidly. In the calm she was a fever. Dawn looked at Eric's hand, the faint scar that went all the way around his wrist. She traced it with her finger. "How'd you get this scar?" she asked. Did he self-inflict too?

"Not a scar. A birthmark. I have it on both wrists." He showed her.

"I know. I saw that. Looks like a scar." She looked

into his eyes, gave him a seductive smirk. "Like maybe you had handcuffs on too tight?" She crawled on top of him, kissed him. Fever. The little candle flame on the nightstand shot up higher.

A sly grin, a little kiss, but he was growing tired. The light in his eyes looked golden. "From a past life maybe." He stroked her hair.

"You are so weird."

"I have a pair of handcuffs in my suitcase. You want me to get them out?" He tickled her.

"Pervert." She tickled him back, and he took her hand in his. He looked at the fading black mark on her hand, the burn and bruise.

"How'd you get this?" he asked but he knew.

"I told you. Moving furniture."

Eric picked the candle up that was on the night-stand, ran his index finger through the flame without burning himself.

Dawn nuzzled into him. "You don't believe me, do you?"

He shook his head, wet his fingers in his mouth, and snuffed out the candle. The room grew a little darker.

"I don't know why I do it, Eric. To feel something. To not feel something. I can't explain it."

"Don't do it anymore. I don't want you hurting yourself."

"I can't help it." She rolled off of him and onto her side. Eric turned to face her, sitting up on one elbow.

"Then I'll help you." He pulled her against him, kissed her forehead. "I won't let you do it. I'll keep my eye on you always." Eric stretched and climbed out of bed. He went about the room putting out the candles, and Dawn admired his naked backside.

"You have a cute behind."

He covered it playfully. "Stop looking at my

tooshie." He crawled back into bed, and she rested her head on his shoulder.

"Did you really mean what you said tonight? That we belong together. Do you really mean it?"

He recited:

Over and over
again
You will see Me.
The eternal hearth
unstoppable love
to ignite and consume
You!
I do not set.
I do not rise.
I am always There
bringing You warmth
bringing You light.

"Is everything a poem with you?" she teased.

"Yes, but an answer too."

"You and me are so different."

"We aren't so different, Dawn. Maybe different experiences but both lonely. Neither of us feeling like we belong in this messed up world."

"I've never thought of it that way before." The room was in darkness, but Dawn felt safe. The warmth in her soul was finally stable. "I feel like I belong now ... with you ... and it's not so lonely anymore." She unleashed her burdens and told him about her past (the first time she had ever told anyone so much). "I don't think I've ever received love, nothing you could really call warmth."

"Tell me," he said, the whites of his eyes visible in the dark.

"Mom was harsh. Cold. Hateful. You just

wouldn't believe ... like a mean principle at school or something. Maybe she was bitter. I don't know. The only compliment I can give her is that she turned our wine into a local brand that was as popular with drunks as soda is to caffeine addicts. I kind of think she'd be proud knowing I sold it for a huge profit, but none too happy that it's in the hands of a competitor in Alma."

"Like Pepsi being sold to Coke?"

"Yeah. I'm sure they are all turning over in their graves. Anyway, as for my parents, they were the classic case of the well-to-do meets the ne'er do well. Mom, I guess, felt rebellious back then. My dad worked at the vineyard. He was tilling the field one day and decided to pluck something more than grapes when he took his break. Mom was, you know, rich girl good girl, even though she was stern and hard, she was still like a choice dessert. Before I even popped out of the womb, he was already locked down in jail though, so I didn't know him."

"What he do?" Eric asked.

"My grandfather, he was powerful, said my dad raped her and Morrison Thomas was locked up."

"Whoa. You never saw your dad?"

She shivered. "I saw him once. He eventually got out, but he was always put back in. Petty theft, grand theft, any kind of theft, or assault. Mom never let him come around, because by that time she was well-versed on the Corner Wine image, but when I was sixteen I went to the jail just to see." Dawn nuzzled closer against Eric, told him everything without a tear, dictating precisely like the tick of a typewriter. "He smiled at me, no teeth, just this thin grin that looked like a crooked crack along a sidewalk like an earthquake broke this seam along his face, a fault-line, and it wouldn't go away." She stopped for a moment. "But it wasn't like he was smiling because he saw his long lost daughter. He was ... he leered at me." Dawn pulled the covers a little closer, covered herself completely. Eric's eyes were listening and kind. "His eyes were like this hollow tunnel that went nowhere. It reminded me of my grandfather. You know who he was like?" Eric shook his head. "I was small when he died but I remember him. He was like the Tin Man in the *Wizard of Oz*, but not in a good way. He was grayed all over with skin like clay, and he wore this plastic red heart pendant around his neck. He never got a real heart. He was pure evil." Deep into Eric's eyes, she looked, giving him all the answer he needed. "That's why I believe some people should never come back. Dead should be dead."

For Eric, such stories were only in movies or television melodramas. His whole life people had treated him as if he should walk on rose petals. The world was sunny and bright, even in the darkness, there were stars. A candle was always lit for Eric. And there was magic. He had seen it with his own eyes. But to comfort Dawn, there were no words to use (magical or otherwise), this he knew, and he held her close. He waited a moment for tears that never came and held back his own with a dam that had to be as mighty as the Hoover because his insides – that sensitive vulnerable boy – were about to rupture.

"It's okay, Eric. As they say, we all have our sad stories," she said, nudging him in the stomach playfully. He winced a little. "I deal with it. I think it's worse for you. You lost your parents and you loved them."

"I do miss them."

"Are you going to tell me your story, Mr. Writer?"

"I think your descriptions were quite nice. You could have been a writer too."

"Me? No! Now, go on, tell me your stories. I like talking in the darkness. It feels nice. Snuggly nice."

Eric took a deep breath. "I was born on a cold Alaskan day ... " Dawn giggled. "I walked three miles to school with no shoes uphill in a rainstorm." Dawn giggled again and told him to be serious. "My first memories ... hmmm ... let's see. My dad liked to build stuff. He was an engineer at a car company. He was always tinkering with something around the house, especially cars, but he had an adventurous streak too. Took off on a treasure hunt at age seventeen without telling my grandparents."

"Did he find treasure?"

"He found Mom."

"Ah. That's sweet."

"She was really poor, raising her two brothers and sister. The idea of a treasure – wow – she took off the rest of the way with him with her siblings in tow. She was cool like that. I thought she was superwoman. She could do anything, knew everything, and was beautiful and motherly. She wore a lot of silk so she always felt soft. Mom had this little boutique and sold and repaired vintage clothes. She made most of their competition outfits too, and my parents always looked so dapper. Dad in that top hat and tails, Mom in the glitzy dress. How could you not think your parents were super-people with all that sparkly? When they went out, they glistened!"

"Competition outfits?"

"They were ballroom dancers ... let me correct, *champion* ballroom dancers, mostly swing."

Playfully, she shoved him. "That's how you learned to dance like that."

"I got the rhythm in me."

"So they won trophies and stuff for the dances?"

"Oh yeah. They went all over the world. Kinda famous."

"Cool."

"They met right here in Arkansas actually."

"Really? Do you still have family here? You didn't tell me – "

"Oh no. They're all over the place. Uncle Nate is a rancher in Texas. Aunt Chessie teaches theater in a high school in Florida. My uncle Homer floats around Europe like a hobo."

"Your uncle is a hobo?"

"Just about. It's by choice though. He's a free spirit. He doesn't want an address. I don't see any of 'em much anymore. I sort of did my own thing after Grandma Pilot died, lost contact, over the years it got worse."

"Do they know you're a writer?"

He nodded.

"Do they know you're a famous writer?"

He nodded again. "The last time I saw uncle Homer was in Paris after the publication of my first book. He introduced me to his friends as his 'famous nephew.' I don't feel famous, and I don't want to be. The desire for fame is the desire for strangers to love you. I don't get all that silly stuff that goes with fame." He shrugged. "I don't need a red carpet or a VIP room to make me happy. I hate celebrity. Celebrity killed art. Well, corporations too. Nowadays, celebrity and business validate what is and is not art, but art is about feeling and expression, and neither celebrity nor business have that capacity. They are both about money. I want no part of it. I'm just glad my writing is not smoke – quickly evaporated and never heard."

"Is that why you weren't offended that I didn't know you?"

"It doesn't bother me. Why should anyone know my face over someone else? Besides, for the most part, faces behind books are rarely recognizable, and I think that's a good thing. Daphne du Maurier said writers should only be read and never seen. I agree. They need to stop putting the writer's photo on the back of the book. Have you ever seen an author's photo on a book cover and not wanted to read it? *That's* who wrote it?"

Dawn laughed. "Yes!"

"Scary. I don't want people saying that about me." He stretched, yawned. "Besides, once people get a taste of fame, they turn into something else. It's been my experience that celebrities are all shallow, greedy people who will do anything for attention." He pondered for a moment, thinking about the Rosabelle from his past, and added, "Of course, they were probably that way to begin with."

"Yeah, I think so too."

"I guess some are okay. I don't want to generalize," Eric said. "The ones I have met fit the stereotype though."

"Do you remember that guy Creative Mose?"

"Oh, yeah, that song, *Mr. Dance Dance Pants*. That was so stupid."

"I used to have a crush on him."

"Oh geez! Say it ain't so!" Eric couldn't stop laughing.

"Hey, I was only ten!"

Eric sang, "Dance, dance, shake a ma pants." Eric laughed again. "That was so stupid!"

"I know. But I thought he was cute. Everyone did. It was the early 90s! My mom didn't know I liked him though, but she wanted to impress these clients or whatever, and got tickets to see him in Little Rock, because it was a big deal that he was coming to Arkansas. Mom had a lot of clout so we went backstage to meet him. Mom gave him a Corner Wine gift basket, and I gave him this lollipop flower arrangement that I made myself, just a bunch of different suckers wrapped together with tissue paper."

"You know the line is actually 'suck her flower,' not 'sucker flower'?"

"I was a dumb innocent kid!"

"That's sweet though, that you thought that," Eric said.

"Not sweet. He made me cry."

"That song?"

"No! Afterward, he was walking to the stage, and I happened to be standing alone, Mom hobnobbing or something, and I asked if he liked the present I gave him. He never stopped walking, like he was too good to stop to listen to me. I didn't deserve that common courtesy even. I told him about the gift, and all he said was, 'Nope, doesn't ring a bell.' I had just given it to him!"

"What a jerk! He's the reason people think celebrities are a-holes! I don't want people to think I'm like that."

Dawn pulled the covers closer around him. Her head on his chest now, he flung an arm around her. "You're not like that though."

"No, I try to talk to little girls that approach me. Not that any do, but if they did!"

"Little girls shouldn't be reading your poems! It would kick-start premature puberty!"

He nuzzled into her hair. "Do the poems turn you on?"

She giggled. "Maybe. Aside from the two I've heard you recite, I've only read one. By the way, I never got my free book. You promised me a book." She sat up and looked down at him.

"Oh, yeah," he said, remembering, "It's coming. I'll get you a book. Tell me which poem you read already."

"*Constant.*"

"The sentimental one?"

"You're a real artist, Eric. I bet every girl you've ever liked has loved you back. If you wrote them poems like ... "

Eric sat up too, leaned in close, lips almost touching hers. Dawn ran her fingers through his hair, and he kissed her gently. "John Keats said most women he met wanted to marry a poem, be given away by a novel. Did they really love him?" Eric replied. The little candle on the nightstand beside them still had a faint ember. Eric rolled onto his back and put his arm above his head. "There is love, there are crushes, infatuations, there are 'compatible couples,' but there is only *one* beloved, one soulmate, one other half." Eric snuffed the candle out again with his fingertips. "It's late. Let's sleep now."

"No, Eric, I want to hear it. Tell me. Why do you believe in these things? That poem you wrote, it's like you were ... talking to me."

He rested on one elbow. Smiled. Yes. "You promise to listen with an open heart and mind?"

She nodded. His face bright in the darkness.

"You want to know why I believe in magic? I've never told anyone before."

"I want to hear."

"Buttermilk."

"Excuse me?"

He took a deep breath, sat up cross-legged. The moonlight cast a warm glow over his face. "It started with tragedy. I was just a little boy, lost my parents, and six months later my grandfather died. I was bitter. So bitter." He shook his fists. "I was a nuclear bomb ready to go off. It would take a miracle to make me believe in anything magical. I was headed down the path to a cold heart of steel until my grandfather's funeral. For me, and my grandmother, it was magic, what happened that day." He recounted the tale to Dawn, who listened like someone immersed in a good book, ready to turn the page to learn more.

On that very cold day in Alaska, Grandma Pilot had explained, "Death, Eri, a mere magic trick, just like the tricks Grandpa always showed you. Metamorphosis. The person in the box doesn't really disappear. Death is that same kind of trick. You don't see that person anymore, but they're still around."

Little Eric had looked about the room, gotten off the bed, looked under it, picked up his blanket, looked under it, too. Grandma Pilot had smiled, knowing even in that childish moment, he would be a believer. "You'll see them again some day," she had said, patted the bed for him to return. "Remember I told you that after Mama and Papa died."

"Yes. I'll see Mama, and Papa, and Grandpa Pilot again, but when?"

Somehow that little boy knew, understood, but in a way that any child believes in the Easter Bunny or the Tooth Fairy. When he witnessed it with his own eyes, the flame within him ignited, burned for a reason he was too young to fully understand then. But he knew now and he told every detail to Dawn.

As they had stood in the funeral home, Grandma Pilot fixing Eric's tie, he waited for the "sign," the little bit of magic between his grandparents. To some, what transpired next was but a funny coincidence, nothing more, but to Eric it was a sign that his grandfather loved his wife so much that he could send her a message from beyond the grave. Just like magicians, Grandma Pilot had explained, the dead can use code words to conjure their magic. It doesn't have to be abracadabra or alakazam. Buttermilk is just as good. Maybe even better because only the two involved understand the secret code.

It was a simple enough message. Grandpa Pilot loved buttermilk. Drank it every morning for breakfast, had a glass every night before bed. When he had sat in his rocking chair for the last time, the night of his death, he had looked at his wife – she already knew it was coming – and said "Buttermilk." She was about to get up to get him a glass when he stopped her. "No," he had said, "you'll know it's from me, if you hear that word. It has to be completely random, ridiculously random."

"People don't drink buttermilk anymore," she had said, sitting in his lap for the very last time.

"I know," he had told her. "That's why it'll work."

So, Grandma Pilot had explained to Eric on that day, very simply and warmly (although inside she was burning with sadness), "All great lovers have a code so they'll know one another, when they meet again, or when they pass on. It has to be something that only those two understand. A word, a phrase, whatever they want. But it must arrive naturally, can't be forced. They can't tell anyone else, but I'm going to tell you, because I know you'll keep our secret." Even though they were alone, she still had whispered in Eric's ear, "Buttermilk."

Young Eric's eyes were watchful, his ears alert. Looking for buttermilk. He wanted that code just as much as she. As they were about to enter the funeral, he had seen the coffin. Sure enough his grandfather was dead. Just one coffin this time. His parents had rested side by side, Everett's pale blue, Harmony's coffin shiny pink. Eric did not want to go in. He forgot about code words and magic. Grandma Pilot had let him cry until they both saw something so bizarre they could not help but stare. A bride and groom entered the church holding hands.

"I think you want the church across the street," Grandma Pilot had said. "This is the Pilot funeral."

"I'm so sorry," the bride had responded, embarrassed.

"Forgive us the intrusion. We're both a little nervous today," said the man, who had a gentlemanly voice like his father. Before they left, he looked down at Eric and asked, "What's that behind your ear, little boy?" Eric had smiled sheepishly, embarrassed, felt around his ears. The groom had walked over, pulled a quarter from behind Eric's ear.

Not meaning to sound smug, Eric had replied, "My

grandpa can do that too. He taught me how."

"It's a classic." He gave Eric the coin.

Eric had played with the quarter, lost in his memories of Grandpa Pilot, tossed the coin up and down.

"He's so cute. Is he your grandson?" the bride had asked.

Grandma Pilot nodded.

"Who passed on?" the groom asked.

"My husband."

Feeling silly in a wedding gown, about to start her own married life, the bride blushed a little, but her betrothed asked politely, "How long were you married?"

"Forever."

The man had nodded. Smiled. Understood. "That's a long time. Now, I do plan to stay married to this pretty young lady that long if, and only if, she keeps buttermilk in the fridge at all times."

Eric dropped the quarter and looked up. The quarter rolled to Grandma Pilot's feet; she reached down to pick it up.

"Buttermilk! Who drinks that? Can you believe it?" the bride had asked, astonished.

"I can," Grandma Pilot had said. And so could Eric.

After telling the story, Eric took another deep breath; he felt a little deflated when he looked at Dawn, who had a quizzical look on her face. He laughed and said, "Guess you had to be there." He lay back down, pulled the covers around them both, waited for her to say something.

"Buttermilk?"

"Yeah. Look, I know to others it was a coincidence, and that's fine because it wasn't meant for them, but for my grandmother, and me, it was so much more." He stroked Dawn's face. "It made her feel better. In that way, alone, it was magic." He had a faint smile on his face. Dawn nodded. He continued, "That's the kind of love I've been after.

A love so powerful that it can send a message from the grave." In his mind he heard the words to *Rosabelle*, but he was starting to grow too tired to talk. "Let's sleep now," he said, rubbing his stomach. "I think I ate too much bread of the dead. My stomach feels sick."

Dawn kissed his chest, watched it rise and fall. "Do you really have to go next week? Can't you stay? The book tour is over, right?"

"I can go wherever I want." He said the words quietly, sleep taking over. His mind was foggy, dreamlike.

"Eric, I don't want you to leave. Are you listening?"

"I'll come back."

"When? You're not listening."

He muttered a response. His eyes were closed.

"If something ever happened to you, I'd want you to come back too. You can't ever die. Promise."

Eric's eyes popped open. "Why would you say something like that?"

"You're jumping out of a plane!"

He glanced down at the top of her head and stroked her hair. "Don't say such silly things. I'm not going to die. Just a trick." Eyes closed.

"Are you going home to Rosabelle?"

Eric opened one eye, snickered. "Dawn, go to sleep."

Eric closed his eyes, fell asleep quickly, but Dawn stayed awake, watching the candle that Eric had snuffed out re-ignite by itself. She whispered, he did not hear, "Please don't leave me," because her days had been too long. Lost in the brief moment of dreamland, Eric was blinded by the euphoric heat within, not realizing he was about to melt, and not via love and lust, the very one he had searched for his entire life. Now that their love had blossomed, he was careless and did not listen.

Dreams

For so many years, Dawn had a burr in her heart that poked her insides like a pine cone rubbing against Saran Wrap. It always hurt when she made a move romantically. She feared that pain like a child afraid to sleep after a scary movie. There would be a nightmare for sure. Eric did not have such nightmares, and he ignored Dawn's apprehensive state on this early October morning, as he lathered grape jam over a biscuit and ate heartily, disregarding the crumbs that dropped onto his lap and the nausea that was growing in his gut. They had just made love again before breakfast, a quiet lovemaking of gentle coos and soft moans. He finally glanced at Dawn, who was only pecking away at her breakfast. "Not hungry?"

"I'm worried."

"About what?"

Dawn rolled her eyes. "Gee, can't imagine. Could it be that you're jumping out of a plane?"

"I've done it before."

"In handcuffs?"

"Well, no ... "

She took a sip of tea.

Eric grinned. "You hold your pinky out ladylike."

"I do not," she said, realizing she was holding the cup with a pinky sticking out the side. Dawn put the cup down. "Don't jump today. You're making a spectacle. Why did you have to call the newspaper? We just had that conversation last night about fame! I thought you hated media attention?"

"I do but Houdini did crazy stunts like this all the time – "

"He was Houdini!"

There was only a slight pause and then he said it, calmly, as if he had asked her to pass him the newspaper. "I am Houdini, Dawn." Those words did not come out of his mouth in exactly the way he had imagined. It was a delicate thing to reveal – like the Wright Brothers admitting they wanted to invent a flying machine in a time when only birds soared. It caused a quizzical look on the face of most. Eric had said it only once before. When he was a boy, he had eventually told his grandmother that he was the great magician, and he would not rest until he found his long-lost bride. The reaction had not been what he expected. Even his beloved grandmother, the believer in all things mystical, had been troubled by his statement. "Eri, it's fine to believe in magical things, but to think this," she had said, perplexed. However, a psychiatrist had deemed young Eric more than sane. Somewhere in a dusty file in a Fairbanks medical clinic, little Eric's old paperwork had the words "genius-level IQ" and "highly imaginative" written and circled in red ink. Instead of being doped up with medications and riddled with ridiculous explanations for his behavior, Eric was allowed to skip two grades and was smart enough to never mention being the reincarnation of Harry Houdini to anyone ever again. He would only say it to one other person, and now she sat staring at him with that same bewildered look his grandmother had years ago. Had he been wrong?

In Dawn's mind, it had not been conceivable that Eric might be insane. To her, he was a very together writer, cool, calm, collected. Insane? No. Quirky and original? Yes. Not crazy. The burr in her heart jutted against her. He could not be insane.

"Why do you think that?" she asked.

Eric shrugged. "I just do."

"Is it that 'buttermilk' stuff – "

"A dream."

"This is about a dream?" Sympathetic.

"I know how it sounds, to you, to anyone, but this was a sign for me. When I was a little boy I dreamed that I was on the ground, shackled with cuffs on my hands and couldn't escape. In the distance, a small woman, slowly came into view. I swear she had a halo around her entire body like a fine mist of smoke, something glowing in the background like fire. She said to me, in a soft-spoken voice, 'Houdini, you dropped your key. I found it in the grass.' She found this key for me, which I think was symbolic and all, so with these dainty hands, she unshackled me. Then, and this is the strangest part, I asked her the time. You know, just said, 'What time is it?' and that glow around her turned to morning-sun-rising-in-the-sky like a blaze. It was so beautiful. She said, 'Can't you tell?' and started to vanish, her voice only a whisper, but I heard the rest of it, the last thing she said after that, and that last sentence woke me up."

"You think that means – "

"She called me Houdini!"

"It's just a dream, Eric."

"It was more than a dream. It was a sign. But, I admit, I thought I understood her answer to the question all these years, but now I think it means something else." He looked at her intently; he wanted to say more but waited for her response. Did she understand?

No.

"Eric, dreams mean all kinds of things. It's our sub-conscious, nothing more." To her, his rational mind was covered in a thick piece of concrete.

He sighed, pushed his plate away. "You don't get it," he said. Calmly, Eric took a sip of coffee, sloshed it around in his cup for a second or two, but whatever held his emotions in check was about to crack in the center like an overheated crucible. Eric stood, paced around the table, coffee still in his hand. "Is there a logical explanation for everything?"

"I don't know. Usually." She pushed her plate away too. "Don't pace like that."

"Weird things happen in life, Dawn. Why can't you accept that? Something weird is happening right now!"

"What's happening, Eric? Sit and finish your breakfast."

He slammed the cup down and it broke. Coffee rushed over the table; Dawn rushed to clean it up, a distraction. "You see, that's you, you'd rather pay more attention to spilled coffee. What's on the surface, nothing beyond it," he yelled.

"Please calm down." Dawn cowered and stopped cleaning the coffee; it spilled on the floor, a waded pile of napkins in the center of the table amongst jagged pieces of ceramic, but the handle was still intact.

"Don't you understand what I'm trying to tell you?" he screamed. Eric felt like he was on the other side of a pane of glass, tapping frantically, to get Dawn's attention.

"I'm not saying anything against your ideas. I don't want you to jump out of the plane. It's crazy. That's all."

"I'm not afraid to take the *death*-defying leap, Dawn."

There was a sharp stab in her heart. All that ice having melted within her wanted to come out in tears but she held it back. Somewhere there were words that would have made sense – I love you – because that's what Eric was really trying to say through his hurt feelings, what he was screaming through that thick wall of glass – but Dawn said nothing, and she would regret having left those words unsaid.

It was no time for a lover's quarrel, and that little bit of hair on Dawn's head that stuck out was a telling sign. It would not stay flat. They appeared to be a stark contrast – Dawn, bright and green, next to Eric in his orange skydiving jumpsuit, borrowed from the pilot Heathcliff Brown. They stood in front of Heathcliff's plane with the crowd before them like a pack of rubber-neckers at a public execution. Maybe he wouldn't make it? It was hodge-podge group of onlookers, families who had come to ride in a biplane, teenagers who had snuck into the hayfields to make out, and oldsters with nothing better to do.

On a card table next to the plane was a single key, casually concealed underneath a bottled water. That was Dawn's job, very simple, to pass him that tiny key, but Eric would not tell her how the trick was done, just told her to slip him the key. "How can you reach your hands if they are behind your back?" she had asked. He had replied, "Trust me. It's a trick," but he had said it snide, as if she were an idiot.

"What you're about to witness, folks," said Heathcliff doing a bad P.T. Barnum impersonation, his look and demeanor just not right for the job, "is an act of – what was the word, Eric?"

"Stupendous." A tape recorder was held like a weapon in front of Eric's face.

"An act of *stupendous* magic." Pouring the spiel on thick, Heathcliff continued, "Folks, this is no small feat. I've seen this done before and most always ... " He rubbed his goatee for an effective pause. "Well, it's never been done either properly or successfully."

"Is that true?" Dawn whispered to Eric. He rolled his eyes.

"Eric Pilot, the greatest poet of our generation, will jump from my plane, *handcuffed*, with only moments, *seconds* I should say, to release himself in time to open his chute."

The reporter who had interviewed Eric for the newspaper, still mad that he had spurned her advances and had not answered her questions about Rosabelle, said in a snide voice, "I think it's an act of *stupendous publicity*. Book sales a little slow?" The crowd chuckled.

"No," Eric said, quietly. He looked at Dawn but she would not make eye contact.

"Can you speak up, Mr. Pilot?" the reporter asked.

"Not publicity. Not at all."

"What then? It's a ridiculous stunt for a *writer*. You're not Houdini."

Dawn took a step back, bumped into the card table, and knocked the bottled water over. As she quickly recovered the water, keeping the key hidden with her hand, Eric said, "I'm doing it to impress a girl." Amid the expected and typical hoots and hollers, he continued, "Although she does consider this an act of stupendous *stupidity*."

The reporter nudged a photographer to take Dawn's photo. "Is that your infamous lady friend?" the reporter asked, less snide, happy to get the scoop.

Dawn squeezed the little key tightly in her hand, closed her eyes, but Eric said only, "She's my lucky charm." Dawn's cue. The onlookers broke into more silly swooning. Covertly, Dawn slipped the key into her mouth, and Eric gave Heathcliff a little nod.

"Lucky indeed," said Heathcliff, securing Eric's parachute onto his back. "I'd give that girl one last kiss just to be safe."

"One last kiss? Heathcliff, you make it sound like I won't make it."

Dawn looked away. It wasn't funny and she felt ill, but Heathcliff handcuffed Eric's hands behind his back and the show was on. Eric feigned discomfort and showed the cuffs to the crowd. People craned their necks and stood on tip-toes to see better. The children in the crowd locked hands excitedly with their mothers or fathers. Teenagers nervously snickered. Heathcliff jumped into the cockpit, started the engine, and the propellers whirled. With his back to the crowd, and in a whisper for Dawn alone, before she kissed him and slipped the key into his mouth, Eric said, "It's no time for fighting. Forgive me?" With that she kissed him, and in what seemed like sweeping movements, Eric was in the plane and in the air.

As the plane went higher, the crowd went wilder. It was all quiet for Dawn. She just watched that little plane get smaller until she could barely see Eric crawl out and stand on the wing of the plane. It too happened just as quickly – he jumped, the crowd yelled out in excitement.

Dawn was the only one who saw it – the key falling from his mouth. At first she thought it was her imagination, but she saw it glinting, falling fast toward the ground. Eric's hands were still cuffed behind his back. The key tumbling. A tiny piece of metal that meant so much falling through the emptiness. The crowd did not see the look of horror on Dawn's face as she rushed to the middle of the field. She wasn't sure what she could do. Catch the little key? Catch Eric? She ran as fast as she could but it was like running through thick mud, although the ground was very solid, fresh cut grass. Alone she stood. For her it seemed like minutes, hours, days passed. She could not look up. She could not look down. Only straight ahead. It was the only way. Then she heard the little clink and looked down. The key was at her feet. Right there at her feet. What were the chances? Shimmering. In the grass. A single key. Weird things did happen. Of all things, why this? That fateful meeting on a train. Real. The nightmare real too? Why? If those magical things Eric talked about were true, why this? Why this now?

Faintly, she heard the crowd behind her, but it was muted like a television set being turned down low. They seemed to be approaching. They were yelling. Were they screaming? All she saw was the key. Senses lost on that one image, unable to see or hear anything else. Everything else around her was haze like a smeared painting. The throng of people pushed against her; she was like a brick wall, but she gave way and looked up.

Eric's parachute was open.

Her knees buckled. She nearly fainted. The crowd ignored her and surrounded Eric in hugs and pats on the back when he landed a few feet away. Eric twirled the handcuffs on a finger; someone asked if they could have them. Eric shook his head. They were all caught up in the thrill, but Eric was not; he noticed that Dawn's face was ghost white, kneeling in the grass.

"Dawn, I'm alright," he said, pulling her up and embracing her. Without any words, she reached down and picked up the little key. She showed it to him. Eric's face went white too. "Oh, Dawn, I never meant for you to see that. You must have thought ... oh, Dawn, I'm sorry."

Someone in the crowd, watching them closely, snickered, "He had a key."

Eric ignored that person, held Dawn and let her cry. While the onlookers rushed home to tell their friends about the crazy plane-jumping poet, Heathcliff cornered the newspaper reporter after landing the plane, kept her from talking to Eric.

"How could you get the parachute to open? That's all I could think of!" Dawn said, as Eric led her away.

"I was never in any real danger. I told you that I've sky-dived plenty of times."

"I thought you ..." She had to pause because the words were coming out in sputters like a car trying to turn over on a cold day. " ... were going to die."

"But I'm fine. There's no need to cry now."

She looked up at him. "How did you do it?"

"Here look," he said, jiggling the handcuffs, showing her a release button. "I was going to show you after it was over. They aren't real handcuffs. Besides, I could reach the ripcord handcuffed. People didn't even realize that. They get caught up in the spectacle and they don't think."

"It was a trick?"

"Of course. You knew that. I told you. There's always a trick to it."

"You made me give you that key just to make *me* think ... and the key had nothing to do with it. You weren't trying to trick the *crowd*; you were trying to fool *me*!" Her heart turned to stone again like lava hitting the cold ocean. A pad lock clamped over her heart. She looked into his eyes – that damned flicker of red-gold-then-orange. Dawn threw the little key on the ground. He did not pick it up.

"I wasn't trying to deceive you, Dawn. I was going to show you how I did it."

"It was cruel."

"You weren't suppose to see that key falling – "

"It doesn't matter. Why didn't you let me in on the secret? Why trick me?"

"I wanted to see if you could guess how I really did it. There's a logical explanation for everything, right?"

Her heart ripped open, seeping into her face, so red. With her fists balled up, she hit him in the chest with such force it nearly knocked the wind out of him.

Not what he expected.

"Are you still mad about this morning?" he asked, catching his breath, but Dawn's heart was shriveling up like a raisin. Eric was trying with all his might to inflate it again. "I said I was sorry."

"There's a logical explanation for everything? Yeah. I'm mad."

"I never meant to hurt you. I wanted to impress you."

"You didn't," Dawn answered with snake venom oozing from her lips like bile congealing in the stomach. "Your so-called stupendous magic does not impress me."

"Come on, Dawn."

"I'm going home." She turned and walked away, without a train car to hide inside.

For a few seconds Eric stood there. He felt like someone had just slapped him across the face, stunned and disoriented. "Don't walk away over something like this," he finally said, running after her with his parachute still trailing behind him. He caught up to her and spun her around. "You're being silly."

She shrugged, folded her arms across her chest.

With his usual assuredness, he said, "You belong with me. You said it too! Our meeting at the train station was not chance, Dawn. Seeing each other every day at the Rosabelle. Of all places – "

"Don't bring up Rosabelle. You won't even tell me who she is," she said, turning her back to him.

"It's a song, a song that – "

"A song, yes, you said that." Terse. She faced him again.

"Bess Houdini was singing that song when she met Harry."

"And that means something to you because you're Houdini?"

He nodded, lost in hope, and did not notice Dawn's

snide inflection, but he was sweating underneath his sky-diving jumpsuit. "It was their secret code word. Like buttermilk. The message Houdini tried to send from the grave was 'Rosabelle, believe.' I put a reference to Rosabelle in my books in hopes that my beloved would see it and know me. It would be a sign for her."

For a brief moment Dawn felt pity for him. Then she felt pity for herself. She had fallen in love with a crazy man. She could not blame him. He was insane. She was clearly the one who had chosen unwisely ... again. The pine cone rubbing against her heart jabbed deeply.

"I'm leaving, Eric."

"Why?" To him, Dawn's logic was a thick layer of concrete that blinded her. How could he knock it down and make her see? A little drop of rain landed on his forehead, and he remembered something from the first moment he had met Dawn. "You're afraid of thunderstorms," he said, his own heart pumping wildly (no burrs to poke him). "Rain clouds follow you. Little black cloud above your head." He pointed upward. The sky had been sunny, and a dark cloud was above them now.

She gave him a dirty look, eyes like slits. "Don't talk in metaphors." Rain started to fall around them, a little sprinkle, making drip-drip-drip noises on his parachute behind him.

"You know what I mean. Storms ruin your sunny day. They always have."

"And you're here to chase it away?" She took off her glasses, wiped away the drops of rain.

"I won't hurt you."

She put her glasses back on, looking at him intensely. "Why should you be any different from everyone else?"

"I'm your beloved. The one."

A downpour. Heathcliff had already taken refuge

with the reporter and photographer in Mr. Colbert's barn. The wings of the plane swayed like a see-saw.

She took her glasses off again. "It's raining. I'm going. I can't see in this."

"I know you can't," Eric said and grabbed her by the arm, made her stay. The rain soaked his hair, drenched his face, and he yelled through the wind, "You can't see anything! Even the things right in front of you! Look at all the signs!"

"Eric, there are no signs!" she yelled back, the wind like an echo. "That stuff isn't real!"

He rolled up his sleeves. "These scars on my wrists, like handcuffs! My name being Eric, Houdini's name being Ehrich. You working on Houdini documents. Living on Rahner Street! Rahner of all places! That was Bess' maiden name. Your middle name is Beatrice, for Pete's sake! You and Bess both collect dolls! Our first date at a theater that Houdini once performed at."

"Eric, none of that means anything. We have to get inside!"

"How can you not see this?" He stomped his foot on the ground like a child, splattering mud and grass.

She pulled away from him. "See what, Eric?"

"I'm Harry and you're Bess." His voice was soft. She had to be Bess.

Just as fast as the rain had come, it suddenly stopped. The cloud was still there, the wind still whipping about, but the rain held back. "I'm not the reincarnation of anyone. I'm Dawn Corner. You're Eric Pilot. Period."

"Dawn, how can you say that?"

"Because it's the truth. Listen to yourself, Eric."

"I've been waiting my whole life to find you. I've never told anyone else. I've been faithful."

"Faithful?"

"There have been other girls but only in my quest to

find you."

Somewhere inside Dawn the rain had stopped too, but from her words Eric did not know it, even though she said with compassion, "Eric, you believe in these things because you can't accept death. You've lost a lot of people you love, and you don't want to let them go."

"This isn't about death. It's about living."

"You have to accept that your parents and grandparents are dead. They aren't coming back."

He ran his hands through his wet hair, squeezed a few locks in desperation, pulling on them. "You don't get it! That doesn't make any sense! This doesn't make sense!" He was as deflated as the parachute hanging from his back. With a quiet, tired, loving voice, he said simply, "I love you, Dawn."

"Are you sure? Or are you following a sign?" She pulled a wet strand of hair from his forehead, and he slapped her hand away. "This isn't love, Eric. It's your obsession. You love me because you think you're suppose to."

In this overcast moment, neither saw a fog, nothing dreamlike. Their vision, like the brightening sky, seemed clear. The look in his eyes now was so warm (not burning) and so solid (no flickering) and so sad (no crackling) that it was hard for Dawn to pull away.

Vision

Eric was in bed with a mask over his eyes. He liked to sleep that way sometimes when he felt lonely. It was an idea he got from Houdini; however, Eric was not sleeping. He was hiding. His heart was like a child holed up under the bed to escape a monster in the closet. Eric closed his eyes tight; if he can't see it, it won't hurt him. At a book signing once, just before he had turned thirty, a woman told him that she used to hide under the bed as a child whenever someone visited their house. She had panic attacks and anxiety throughout her life. Eventually, she went to see a therapist, and in the waiting room there was a book of poetry. She had opened to his, one about destiny. She had liked it, but thought nothing much of it, until the doctor emerged with his hand held out. "It was your poem," she had said. "I knew it was a sign. I understood it in a flash. I had been hiding under the bed all those years so he could pull me out." They were married a year later.

Somewhere in our hearts we know our destiny. It guides our entire life. Many people ignore the call, but the voice, loud or soft, is still there. But Eric wondered, as he stared at blackness, how do we know for sure? While he saw nothing with his eyes at that moment, his ears still heard Dawn's voice, "This isn't love, Eric."

Wasn't it?

To define love, poets and philosophers have tried forever. Eric was sure he knew more than most. He knew what type of "romance" he did not want and had coined a term, "interchangeable relationships." He had used it once during a talk show. "It's the idea that people are as interchangeable as a brand of sliced bread," he had said. "You can pick any slice to make a sandwich. They all work just as well." It's the type of relationship you are told to hope for at online dating sites. It's the kind of relationship you "work at." It's the grownup version of love. There are hundreds of compatible people. It could be anyone. Eric had no use for "compatibility" or any of that nonsense, and few in the audience that night had understood what he had meant.

When it got right down to it, Dawn and Eric had no business being together. She was cold. He was hot. He was light; she was dark. She was trapped in a corner; he expanded like air. But they were not exactly opposites either – two different things that went together like pink and purple. Orange and green.

Eric rolled over onto his stomach; it made the pit in his gut feel a little better. Early morning, raining softly, and although he had not eaten since the day before, he felt extremely nauseated. He reached for the phone and called room service, but not to order food. Eric wanted wine; he lied to himself that he wanted to be drunk, but he really needed something that had been a part of Dawn, sour or not. After the plane jump, he had waited in the field while Dawn walked home alone. At first, he had done nothing, an orange dot in a field of green, then Eric had walked to Dawn's apartment, but she would not answer the door.

Mrs. Crumper had come up to him, as he sat outside in the garden, staring up at Dawn's window, and had quietly clipped the parachute hanging from his back with garden shears.

Soon he would be drunk – he rolled onto his side – but he would not be able to sail through an abyss of ambivalence. Eric could never do that. The thoughts would continue to rumble through his mind like a train, as visible and real as the red flowers he had picked with Mrs. Crumper's permission and had left outside Dawn's door, the way someone might leave flowers on a grave.

"We had flowers like this growing wild on our ranch," Eric had said to Mrs. Crumper for something to say. The cool writer was gone; he was crushed like a tin can. "My grandfather had hay fever though," he had continued, and Mrs. Crumper made him licorice root tea and had listened to his stories. "They're both dead now. My parents too. I know that, but I like to think they are still with me. Maybe I am delusional? Maybe Dawn's right and I have a problem accepting death?"

"Everyone has a problem accepting death, dear," Mrs. Crumper had said. "Every religion has a concept of the afterlife, whether they believe in heaven, hell, or reincarnation. Not a single one thinks dead is dead. If accepting death is a mark of sanity, then we are all delusional."

He had nodded.

"But that's not what's really bothering you, is it, dear?"

"Maybe I don't understand love. The writer of love poetry and he doesn't get it himself."

"Dear, there's nothing to understand. Either you love or you don't. It doesn't take a poet to figure that out." She had given him a warm hug, but it was a long time before Eric stopped staring at Dawn's window and left the garden.

In his hotel room, Eric padded to the door, rubbing his side. A friendly attendant smiled when Eric opened the door. "I saw you in the paper this morning," the person said, and Eric gave a weak grin. He rolled a cart into Eric's room with a bottle of red wine and two glasses (his heart sank, he only needed one). After one autograph and a tip, Eric slumped down on the sofa. He couldn't see the sun, but it was lighter outside, the rain only a sprinkle. The storm was over.

When the Sunday evening storm had begun, Eric had sat outside the Rosabelle, not inside, because there had been a woman in his regular spot talking on her cell phone. For awhile, Eric had taken a seat on a sofa. The woman had an empty plate in front of her and was talking, very seriously and loudly, to a romantic partner. A lovers' spat, but Eric saw no love emanating from the woman's words. "What are we going to do?" she had kept yelling. The man had lost his job. "I can't do this," the woman had said after much deliberation and hung up. What the woman "couldn't do," Eric knew, was live in uncertainty. Most people coupled up for companionship or obligation, many times out of fear of destitution, whether it be loneliness or security. Not love. This woman had a relationship of necessity, and her loyalty stayed with the supplier of those needs. She was like a fan at a baseball game. She cheered for whoever hit a home run. Her boyfriend had just struck out and there was no putting him back in the game. And, Eric reasoned, there was no reasoning with her, because some people did not see the fire. They had no concept of passion. It was like a color-blind person. They would never see red.

Dawn could see, but she kept her eyes closed. Her road was lit, but she moved along a straight path, never veering off, using the same map as others before her, others would use after her, others were using at that very moment.

Fear drove her too. Not Eric. He drove and foraged with purpose, a traveler who looked at the signs and steered to what interested him.

As he sat in his hotel room drinking his wine, he removed the skydiving jumpsuit (slept in all night). His T-shirt and jeans were soaked underneath from sweat, but it had kept him dry when he had sat outside the Rosabelle, annoyed by the ranting woman who would not leave his favorite spot. At first, there had only been dark clouds, but in a matter of seconds Eric was sitting on the sidewalk in a downpour just like the one that had happened in the field. People had ran past, but a few had looked. Is that a tear? Or a raindrop at the corner of his eye? There had been strong wind, and it had loosened the hinges of the sign above the café door. Eric had watched it blow topsy-turvy above his head before taking a cab back to his hotel and crashing into bed. Loudly. His stomach hurt.

Still. More wine. More wine. More. His thoughts turned sour. Dawn was a rich girl sour girl annoying girl baby girl mean girl unloving girl – an angry cloud unleashing her rain whenever she got scared.

Eric's stomach hurt more, and he went to the bathroom and threw up. He stumbled and looked at himself in the mirror. America's Most Handsome ... and he had a dribble of vomit in the corner of his mouth. Eric wiped it away, took a shower, and went down to the bar. More wine.

He was sufficiently inebriated, blurry eyed, when the front desk clerk, who was on a break, asked him, hopeful, "Did you get a chance to see all the sights in Hot Springs, Mr. Pilot?" Eric nodded. She sat beside him. "Even Magic Springs?" He shook his head, puzzled, sobered up a little. He rubbed his eyes. Magic? What had he missed? She explained, happy to have his attention, "It's an amusement park. They're only open a few more

days this year since summer is over. My season pass al-
lows me to bring a guest." Eric looked at her, really looked
at her, noticing every freckle on her cheek, the way her nip-
ples showed through her uniform, her slender neck, delicate
hands with polished fingernails. Her legs were long like a
model. Small waist. Small feet. She arched her back
when she sat, kept her breasts pointed out, and dangled her
shoe off her foot with her legs crossed. She was pretty. He
hadn't really noticed that before. But he did not love her,
not even in the slightest most physical lustful way. Eric
said nothing in return.

"Well," she said quietly, standing, "I hope you enjoy
your last day here." She started to walk off, but turned
back. Eric was about to order a drink when she said something queer. "I've read all your poems. I know what Rosabelle means." Eric's eyes went wide. She became shy.
That flicker. She started to sweat. "It's about Houdini,
isn't it?"

She knew what Rosabelle meant ... but he did not
love her. Not at all.

He nodded; she smiled and walked away.

Something always shatters the illusion, wakes us
mid-dream back to the thing we call reality, whether it be a
honking car, ringing phone, or alarm clock. It's shocking
like ice. Dawn still had sleep in her eyes, but she watched
the yellow canary on the windowsill and could not shake,
nor understand, that warm look Eric had in his eyes when
she had walked away from him. Dawn fed the bird more
toast, stared out at the clouds shifting and moving away.
Red-gold-then-orange. It had to be an optical illusion. Or
her imagination. It certainly wasn't love.

Outside, the storm had ripped through Mrs.
Crumper's garden without constraint. The mums had fallen
to pieces. Most of the apples had dropped from the tree,

knocking the blossoms to the ground too. A branch without leaves dangled above the bird bath. The overworked rain-gutter poured a thick river of mud, cutting the garden in half. Even Leon had toppled over in the night.

Eric would have toppled over too, if he had stayed any longer. In the field, Eric had pled his case like an innocent man in a straight-jacket, but Dawn was sure she was right about his devotion being misguided. He was not Houdini and he could not escape this confine. Dawn had no key to release him, and she had enough restraints of her own.

Below her on the second floor, an argument was out of control. Dawn smelled the smoke from the man's cigar as it wafted throughout the building. He had just returned home from work, the late shift at a factory that made paper-clips and nails. Dawn could not figure out how those two things went together, other than they both held things to-gether. Dawn also did not understand why the couple stayed together. Once, Dawn had bumped into the woman, who had smiled proudly and proclaimed, "It's our anniversary. Thirty-two years today." Dawn thought it sounded like thirty-two years of brimstone, especially the way they carried on, which happened every few days or so.

Most relationships never had the bliss of story-books. Dawn had never seen one, experienced one. She rubbed her eyes and started to close the window when the canary hopped closer. "Do you want to come in?" she asked, sticking her hand out the window. "There's not much to see in here." The bird did not hesitate, hopping onto her finger. Inside, his little black eyes stared at her for a second then he flew around the kitchen. He landed atop the refrigerator, and Dawn had no intention of catching him. He pecked and fluttered his wings then flew to the counter, walking across the flowers Eric had left the day before outside her apartment. Her eyes started to water.

"It's the cigar smoke below," she said to the bird, wiping her eyes. "Do you hear the crazy arguing?" The bird tilted his head like a dog that is trying to understand, but he flew to the open package of bread instead. Dawn pulled out another piece and watched him stab at the slice with his beak. "They argue all the time, those two, and they have been married thirty-two years. That's a death sentence. I read that some birds couple up for life. Eric thinks people couple up forever. That's too long. Don't you think?"

The arguing duo were the only married couple in the building; Mrs. Crumper seemed to attract lonely singles. There was one widow in her forties who lived on the first floor, but Dawn had never seen her. Mrs. Crumper had gossiped that the "poor thing" always wore black in mourning for her husband killed in a sailing accident. The "poor thing" had held his hand as long as she could from the life raft, as he bobbed up and down like a cork, until a strong wave washed him away. Dawn thought the story sounded phony, too melodramatic to be true. She had accidentally received some of the woman's mail – a magazine called *Romance Fiction Monthly* – and had slipped it under her door. Dawn figured the story came from there.

Dawn never got the appeal of tragic love stories. There was nothing romantic about it. Just sad. She let the bird fly about the apartment and went to the bathroom. As she held the warm cloth against her eyes, she felt bad about bringing up the death of Eric's parents and grandparents. That had gone too far. Maybe it was the truth, and maybe he was insane, but that had been too hurtful. Her eyes were red.

There was a loud crash in the living room. She quickly dried her face, rubbing the tears from her eyes. The doll Bale had given to her was on the floor, face shattered. Playfully, the bird pecked at the silent television (was it a dark window?), oblivious to the crash, to the sad. Her dolls had been her only childhood friends, plastic eyes that only stared, the same expression for every sentence Dawn spoke to them. Playmates in her mind. No flicker. The fall had loosened an eye; Dawn removed it, held it up, maybe brown or blue, only a clear glint that reflected nothing. The doll's head had been hollow. The sharp jagged pieces were in a small pile; its body a few inches away. She couldn't keep a headless doll.

Dawn was about to press a pointed piece into her palm when there was a knock at the door. Too early. Eric? No. The smell of blueberry muffins drifted into her apartment before she opened the door.

"Quite the early bird, aren't we – Yowza!" Mrs. Crumper said, ducking, as the bird zoomed over her head out into the stairwell. "You've got a bird in your apartment."

"Um yeah."

Mitch barked, ran after it.

"It's good luck," Mrs. Crumper said, "having a bird in your house."

"I'll catch him."

"Don't worry 'bout it," she said, making her way inside, holding a tray of muffins. "I'll leave the complex door open. He'll fly out eventually." She yelled to Mitch to come back. Brazen, he plopped down on the sofa. Putting the muffin tray on the coffee table next to Dawn's purse, she sat down and ruffled Mitch's fur. "Don't chase birds, boy. It's not nice." She nodded to the tray. "Have some. I saw your light on and thought it only right to share with another insomniac ... or early-riser." She shrugged her shoulders. "Whatever the case may be."

Dawn sat down. "Mrs. Crumper, I don't feel well. I'm – "

"You do look a bit feverish."

"I'm calling in sick today."

Mrs. Crumper unwrapped the tray of muffins. "I think that's a good idea."

"Yes. I need to go back to bed," Dawn said, hoping Mrs. Crumper would get the hint, hoping she would still leave the muffins.

"Have that boyfriend of yours come look after you."

"He's not my boyfriend."

"Ah. But he's the reason you don't feel well."

Dawn shrugged.

"That young man sat in my garden for hours yesterday waiting on you."

"I saw him." She picked up a muffin, pulled out a blueberry from the top.

Mrs. Crumper walked over to the broken doll and picked up the pieces. "Your little doll broke."

"The bird knocked it over."

She put the pieces on the bookshelf and held the headless body. "You could buy it a new head?"

"No. I don't need any more dolls."

Mrs. Crumper sat back down. "What are you going to do now?"

"Throw it away."

"Eric, love. What are you going to do about Eric? I wouldn't let him get away. He's a rare bird. Those eyes of his, I swear they flicker. Most girls would die to be with him."

"He's not what people think." He's lonely too. Eyes red. Stop it! Dawn ate the blueberry. It had already turned the tip of her finger blue.

"What is he then?"

"A little crazy." She took a big bite of the muffin, chewed it as if contemplating the word "crazy."

"Those are the best kind." Mrs. Crumper said and paused for a moment. "You know what they say about him, don't you?"

Dawn shook her head, but wanted to say she knew the secret of Rosabelle.

"That Eric Pilot isn't even human. He's fire itself. That's how he ignites women so warmly."

Dawn laughed.

Mrs. Crumper smiled. "We both know that's not true. We also both know he's not crazy, maybe crazy with love, but not insane. The man who sat in my garden was definitely human, capable of such intense feelings that some might call madness, but it's far crazier to deny how you feel."

"I don't know if I can look him in the eyes again. I hurt him so badly ... "

Mrs. Crumper waited. Dawn pulled off a huge chunk of the muffin, toyed with it before eating it.

"It's not his feelings that I think are mad," Dawn said. "You should have seen the look in his eyes. It's his ... *belief* ... one belief in particular. He wants me to believe something crazy."

"The relationship hinges on this belief?"

"Well, no, I don't guess so. It's just strange. Mrs. Crumper, if he told this to anyone else, they'd have him locked up in a mental institution."

"Yet he trusted you enough to say it?"

Dawn looked away. "I don't think you understand."

"How strange could it possibly be for you to walk away from that lovely boy?"

"He thinks we're the reincarnation of Harry and Bess Houdini." Crazy laugh. She thought she had stumped Mrs. Crumper finally with that one. She ate the rest of the muffin.

"Maybe you are. Has to be someone."

"No, it doesn't."

"That boy is lucid. You know that, and I know that, and he trusted you with a secret. It must have been hard for him ..." Mrs. Crumper pondered, laughed under her breath, and said softly, finally realizing, "Rosabelle."

"It's a song."

"Yes, I know, and I know that story, but I never would have guessed that. Of course, no one knew Eric thought he was Houdini. That would have solved the mystery early on." She pointed at Dawn with a grin. "You're Rosabelle."

"I'm not. Besides, you can't prove something like that."

"Of course not. Love isn't science."

"For Eric, it is. The science of signs. It's all about what is meant to be and not meant to be. Besides, he's the one who wants proof anyway. Not me."

Mrs. Crumper gave Dawn a hard stare. "Is he?"

"I don't believe in those things."

"But you love him."

Dawn knew it was not a question. "I just met him."

"That changes nothing. You loved him the moment you saw him just like a mother loves a child as soon as it comes out of her. Time means nothing."

"Time is everything. He's leaving tomorrow. I'll never see him again."

"Then you better enjoy today." Mrs. Crumper picked up a muffin and stood. Mitch jumped off the sofa, ran to the door, and waited impatiently. Before leaving, she added, "Don't throw a wet blanket on his fire, love. You'll end up cold."

Outside the sun had freed itself from the clouds. Mrs. Crumper quietly closed the door behind her. Dawn slid off the couch and slumped onto the floor. Holding her face in her hands, she sighed and closed her eyes. Tears.

Eric Pilot. The writer of poetry. Leather-bound books. Smells of maple leaves. Chews licorice gum. Eats marshmallows. Lights candles for dead magicians. No

milk. Keeps a childhood blanket. Dances the tango.
Pocket watch. Wears a fedora. Loves shiny shoes. Loves
... me.

All those things on the good list, one thing that mattered.

Destiny

Alone in the hotel bar, Eric had his leg kicked up lazily over the arm of the chair, reclining back with his eyes closed, face covered with his hat, listening to *The Song Is Ended* by Louis Armstrong and The Mills Brothers as it played over the hotel speakers. He did not see Dawn come up to him.

"You're a cliché, you know," Dawn said faintly.

Eric smiled, did not open his eyes, and shrugged.

"Glass of wine. Old hotel. Listening to 1920s jazz." She tried not to grin, pretending to be serious. "All you need is a sad love story, a couple sheets of paper, and a pen to write it down. A cliché poet."

"I told you clichés are good." He pulled his hat down, opened one eye. "Do I have a sad love story?" She smiled back at him. Eric opened his eyes, put his leg down, and straightened himself up, rubbing his side. Noting the song being played, he asked, "Do you want the love song to end too early?"

"From what I gather from the song, the melody never goes away, even after the tune ends."

He stood up, stumbled a little, and put his hat on.

"That's what I've been trying to tell you." He put his hands on her waist, so warm she shivered. They danced for a moment, her hands lightly touching his chest, feeling the gentle thump of his heart. His eyes were golden.

"I looked for you at the Rosabelle," she said.

"It's not lunch time."

"You're always there."

He smiled. "Shouldn't you be at work?"

"I called in sick."

"Naughty. You look fine to me." When he kissed her, she tasted the wine on his lips.

"Are you drunk?"

"Baby, I'm fried to the hat." He flicked the brim of his fedora.

"You didn't get drunk on my account, did you?"

"Of course."

"You're on the front page of the newspaper this morning. I saw it on the way over."

"So I hear. My claim to fame."

"They called you The Houdini Poet."

"Hey, I like that!"

"I knew you would." She did not tell him that one-fourth of the article was about their argument in the field.

In a partially drunken slur, he asked, "Hey, you want to make love to a magician? I'm famous."

"That's *all* I want to do today."

Eric slung his arm around her shoulder and rubbed his side. "Me too."

"Are you feeling all right?"

"Perfect as can be."

"You seem a little unstable."

"Too much wine." He nodded toward the elevators. "Let's go upstairs. I'll show you my magic wand." He made a little "hee hee" snicker.

"I've seen it."

"Then you'll know that it is stupendous!"

They walked towards the elevators with Eric reclining on Dawn for help. "I think you need to sleep this off first."

"No sleep. Wastes too much time."

Dawn pressed the elevator "up" button. Eric leaned against her with a seductive smirk. "I have serious things to say, Eric. We have to talk first."

"Ehhh, Dawn, listen. I was a careless jerk and scared you ... sometimes I believe things ... I don't stop to consider. But I've learned something."

"No?" she teased. The elevator door opened and they stepped inside.

"What counts," he said, tapping the tip of her nose, "is that I love you."

"Let's just enjoy our last day together."

Whispering into her ear as the elevator doors closed, "What makes you think this is our last day together? I'll come back."

"When?" She pressed the button for his floor.

"I want you to see where I live. Come see Alaska."

"I'll freeze."

He put his hands on her face, felt the warm flush of her cheeks. "Not anymore." The elevator doors opened but Eric did not step out. "I'll go back home, clean the place up a bit 'cause I know you're particular about that, and come back for you. We could get a dog! And a canary! No moo cows."

Doubt.

A knowing look. "I'm not that drunk, Dawn. I know what you're thinking. You don't think I'll come back, do you?"

"I want you to." She pulled him out of the elevator. "I'll go anywhere with you."

"I'll come back. I promise."

Thundering like clouds and shining like the sun, they spent that entire day making love. It may sound a bit too sentimental, but this is a great love story after all, and without sentiment, it would mean something less. A shimmering moment so grand and lovely – the very thing they had both been waiting for their entire lives – destiny – they held it for as long as they could. Sweet minutes – giggling and pillow fights. Manic seconds – hair pulling, names yelled, backs scratched. Tearful times –

Tuesday came too soon. It was starting to get chilly. Raining softly for now. Eric pulled his blanket closer, traced the biplane patch. His eyes were a faint orange glow. A warm ember fading quietly in a fireplace. His hair, wet with sweat, stuck to his forehead. Dawn brushed it back. "Do you really think you're Houdini?"

"I do," he said, feeling cold, and he tried to hide it from her. There was a twinge in his gut, and he felt like a jagged rock was stabbing his insides.

"It's a little off the wall to believe that."

He smiled. "I suppose it is."

"If you're Houdini, why did you become a poet instead of a magician?"

"Done it already." Cavalier.

"It's not something you can ever prove."

"There are a lot of things you can't prove. Doesn't make it less real." He curled up close to her. She nodded, because the bed was warm, life was now warm. "I learned something from you, Dawn Corner. I'll say it again. You made me realize that the best indicator for the eternal beloved is feeling, and I have that in abundance for you. It's irrelevant for you to believe in our reincarnated souls or signs or mystical moments."

"I shouldn't have said the things I did in the field, especially about your family dying."

"Maybe a little truth to it."

"It's okay if you want to believe it," Dawn said. "Even the Houdini stuff. It's okay."

"I guess I am a little obsessed with it." He sighed. "When I found out Bess never got her code, I was sad because it had worked for my grandparents, so it should work for anyone. I guess a part of me thought that if I was Houdini, I could find her and give her the code myself. I've followed signs about that my whole life, thinking it would lead me there. I knew my soulmate was at the other end of that list of clues. Maybe it is crazy?"

"It brought us together, so it had meaning."

Eric smiled. "You think?"

Dawn nodded.

"But there is something really important that you need to know. You think I love you because I'm following signs, but that's not true. I loved you the moment I first saw you at the train station, and I didn't know anything about you. I don't think of signs as the 'reason' for things, but I see them as little clues that I'm on the right path. Disregarding signs is like ignoring a buzzing smoke detector. It goes off for a reason. There were so many clues with you and I followed them."

"I'm glad that you did."

The sun was up but it was dark outside. "It's Dawn," he said, his breath ice.

She nodded, nuzzled against his chest. His skin was hot, but he was shivering, and he could not hide it anymore. Dawn felt his forehead for fever. "Eric, you're sick."

"No, listen to me. It's just a stomach ache. The Houdini dream with the key ... "

Dawn got out of bed. "I'm going to turn the thermostat up. Turn the fan off."

"Just listen," he said in a soft voice. "When I asked her the time, she said, 'It's Dawn.' It wasn't the answer to the time of day ... and you found my key in the grass."

Dawn held her finger on the thermostat control, but did not move it. She crawled back into bed. It was his wilting eyes, not his words. "Your eyes have changed color."

Thunder. Hail stones crashed against the window. His eyes trying to hold on to that glow.

To anyone who walked into the hospital room, Eric had brown eyes. Only Dawn could see the fading glow beyond it now. Both of their skin flushed with fear but neither showed it, protecting the other. He was smiling – the painkiller starting to kick in. The nurse who prepared him for surgery, checking his pulse, reading blinking machines, was oblivious to his once-flickering eyes. Any other patient, he was to the nurse, no more the raging fire that sent women to their knees. That flame of his was now so directional, only towards Dawn, that it was like staring at the depth of a two-dimensional object. He was barely visible to the naked eye.

"I found you," he said, voice clear, happy, but groggy.

"Yes and everything's going to be okay now."

"I have a flair for the melodramatic."

"You do, Mr. Houdini."

He laughed softly at that. "Do you believe me now?"

She shook her head but smiled.

"You want to know something weird?" he asked.

"That wouldn't be a first."

He laughed again then his face went somber. "I never saw this coming. I really didn't."

"Saw what coming, Eric?"

He raised his arms, flapped them around, indicating the hospital room. "All of this." A flash of anger.

"People have their appendix out all the time. I can't

believe you're afraid of a little operation." Dawn kissed his forehead. Cold.

"I'm not, and I'm not afraid of death either."

"Don't even say something like that. You aren't going to die."

He snorted and rolled his eyes.

"People don't die from this."

"Houdini died from appendicitis." Pissed off.

"What?" Fear. But she did not believe ...

"Some coincidence, huh?" Eric said, voice sad. She had never heard his voice so melancholy. "What are the chances?"

"Eric, it's just ... a coincidence, yes."

"On Halloween? You've forgotten, Dawn, he died on Halloween. Today is Halloween."

Before Dawn could ask, as if she felt the question coming, the nurse said, "Now, now, this kind of talk, Mr. Pilot, don't go thinking things like that. Your lady friend is right. People have their appendix out all the time. It's one of the most common cases we get. I've never seen anyone die from it." She patted his shoulder. "Don't you worry now. The doctor will take good care of you. You should be okay."

"*Should*? Then why'd you make me fill out those forms listing my next of kin? If I die, it's not the hospital's fault, et cetera, et cetera ... all that jazz?"

"Hospital procedure."

Eric threw up his hands, rolled his eyes again.

"See, Eric, you're being melodramatic!" Dawn said to the nurse, "He gets like that."

The nurse looked at Eric, as if for the first time. "When we give you the anaesthetic you'll be out like a light in three seconds. Wake up like a brand new morning. Never know what happened, never feel a thing."

Dawn leaned over him and he pulled her close for a

kiss. Still passionate. The nurse politely turned away, pretended to write something down on a clipboard. "Stop freaking me out with this kind of talk, Eric," Dawn said into his ear.

"I thought you didn't believe anyway?"

"Just stop."

Another nurse came into the room, pushing another bed. "Time to go," the woman said to him.

"I'll be here when you get back," Dawn said, holding Eric's hand.

"I know. I've always known."

"Besides, you still owe me a book."

The nurse helped him to the other bed, but he did not let go of Dawn's hand. "Dawn, I have another stupendous magic trick for you. Wait for it. It's a good one." He winked, put his head on the pillow. Dawn's hand slipped from his.

"Eric," she said – the way his name sounded ... Eric! ... still made her smile – and he loved the way she said it ... Eric!!! ... making him grin too – talking to him in a whisper so the nurses would not hear, "I have to tell you ... the stuff about 'Rosabelle, believe' is not important. Signs and codes and coincidences ... don't worry about that stuff. You're going to be okay."

"Is that what you wanted to tell me?" Small smile on his sad face.

She shook her head. Just in case ... this silliness, she tried to remind herself ... but ... he ... he had to know. She felt it ... "I love you, Eric." Loud. Those words, never spoken before, came out easily like the strum of a guitar. So simple. So unbelievably simple and true. She wanted to say it a million times, but there was no more time ...

And he looked at her. That flicker. Red. Gold. Orange. Once more. Then his eyes closed.

Quiet

Quiet.

A quiet so loud it hurt Dawn's ears. Eric's pocket watch was in her hand. She thought the watch was ticking. It was not. Nothing was ticking. Not a single noise. Frozen, the hands, as if the world were on pause. 1:26 p.m. Eric's hat on the back of a chair.

Quiet.

Everything felt like her imagination. She put her hands over her ears.

Quiet.

A fan had been left on. It made no noise. Hadn't it the night before? In his bed now, not moving, not crying. No noises. She kicked the fan over. It sputtered and stopped. Not a single noise. His blanket. The sense of smell. The sense of warm. It was still there. Loudly still there.

So was that gravelly voice of that doctor, who was

suppose to take "good care" of him, and it rang in her ears when he had said, "He listed you as next of kin." That's when her hearing stopped. She wished she had gone blind instead. That doctor had come quietly into the room but she had seen the door open. Tightly she had closed her eyes to stop from hearing, "Sometimes people have a severe allergic reaction to the anaesthetic." Eric's clothes, in a bag, beside her feet.

Quiet.

Her apartment. Quiet. Everything so quiet. Mrs. Crumper came in; Dawn had left the door open. She held a tray of sweets. She had seen it on the news.

Quiet.

Dawn turned, on instinct, not because she had heard Mrs. Crumper come in. "Clouds. You know how you see them, they look like something, then you turn away for just a second, just one little tiny second, and you look back up, and they're gone. Gone. Just gone," Dawn said.

Quiet.

Warm smile as Mrs. Crumper placed the tray of food on the coffee table. "They're still there, just turned to something else, love." But Dawn didn't hear her.
"He didn't leave me a sign to let me know he's okay. Like Bess and Harry. Like buttermilk. Rosabelle, believe. How could he forget that?"
But he had not.

Humming

The kitchen was trashed. A knife in her hand.
Against her wrist. So very soft, his voice, in her ear,
"Don't do it, Dawn." But she wanted to be with him ...
wherever that may be. And if there was no such place,
nothing at all, that was better than the ...

... Buzzing

Hands over her ears. A rumbling truck. Horns
honking. People talking. A crossing guard's whistle. Rosabelle Café. The sign hung, one hinge, dangling. No one
at Eric's table.

Dawn picked up an orange leaf. "Where's my sign,
Eric?"

Ringing in the ear.

Loud.

"You wanted Bess to get her code, but it was ME
ME ME ... me ... you were suppose to ... leave a sign for
me ... "

People walked past, no one holding out a hand for
the girl with a little blood on her wrist, not enough to matter, a little scratch because she had heard Eric, the screaming crying girl who was banished to loneliness once more
... sitting on the sidewalk.

Quiet again.

The orange leaf crushed in her hand. She rubbed it
into the sidewalk. Stained it with her tears.

Green

Non-believers say it is a spot of faded paint – it is green, they say, while she had an orange leaf in her hand (they don't understand) – but the odd green stain on the sidewalk in front of the Rosabelle Café only appeared after Dawn cried outside that window every day at 1:26 p.m. – the time of Eric's death (the time of Houdini's) – through fall, through winter. In spring, she stopped coming. The leaves turned green, you see. The sky stayed sunny.

She had made the decision early on. She would go to Alaska ... some day. It had been their plan, and she wanted to see his house. His uncle, the rich rancher in Texas, had said it would be okay. But, she could never get up the courage. It would not make Eric return. For a long while she had been angry. Eric had lied. Promised not to die, promised to return, told her to believe in signs and all manner of magical things. Yet he was dead and she had no sign to comfort her – those silly ideas, she knew for certain were untrue, just as Bess had proven years ago. There are no stupendous magic tricks.

It had been an early morning, March 3rd, Eric's

birthday she later learned, and Dawn stayed in bed and dreamed of Alaska. Every night she had slept with Eric's blanket, not unraveling it like he had as a child (although with one swift pull, she might have fallen apart). The blanket was the only thing that had kept her warm, because Dawn was dead too, although her heart beat and her lungs rose, she took in no air and no blood flowed. Most of the day, she stared not at the ceiling, but nothing. Life was fog. No lighthouse to guide her through darkness. Mrs. Crumper, stumped by these tragic events, could not bring her light, nor could Will and Sledge, who visited her often. Now, technically, she never quit her job at the museum. She just stopped going to work. It was a long time before ... the day everything turned green. The day Eric visited her in a dream.

She wanted to stay there, in that dream, his memory clear as day, but in this dream Eric had invited her to his home, and when she reached for him, Eric had turned to dust. For comfort that morning she took out her childhood dolls, no real reason other than that, just to remember ... and for a moment to forget. She had packaged them up after Eric had died with a few other mementoes she had kept from her train caboose back home; she could not stare at their soulless faces anymore. She wondered what had become of her train car. Wondered if the grapes were ripe. These thoughts, all a ruse, to keep her mind elsewhere. But like great magic, the distraction gives way, and we turn our heads and see it – right there, something impossible, something wonderful. At the bottom of a box of dolls was a book. Dawn had forgotten she had it, forgotten she had kept it. A child's biography about Houdini. Her first reaction was to cry. It reminded her ... She could hear his voice in her head – the sound of it had never faded – "See, Dawn, that is quite the coincidence, don't you think?" The smell of the book was musty, a layer of dust, and she blew it away. The spine cracked like brand new. The first page ... an inscription ...

Rosabelle, believe. Eric Pilot. A drawing of a little airplane.

It was the handwriting of a child but Eric's handwriting for sure. She could hear him laughing ... somewhere. His magic was indeed stupendous. At that moment her eyes went black. That flicker. In her own eyes.

Red-gold-then-orange.

Green, the leaves outside. Her beloved – well, she knew for certain that he was an orange leaf. Some day he would be green again. Dawn believed this completely. See, she had good reason too. She believed in magic. Not something normally associated with a logical woman like Dawn Corner, but that woman was buried by a simple phrase, sent to her from a magical man who was not shackled by time ...

{The Poetry of Eric Pilot}

Constant

I am the fire in the distance.
The constant state of arousal.
Girl with mottled vision through frigid thought,
See me, a light house. Glowing. You
are cold like funeral black. You
desire to be warm, for your breath to be a fever. You
covet the flush on your skin. You
will
melt at *my* touch, liquid and changed. You
Walk toward me. I
am the all-consuming fire. Desire. We
are

waiting
for You.
I will wait
even if certain You
will never come.
But I will always see You
in the distance,
a wind so swift,
brought by the currents of a storm, You
can fuel Me or destroy Me, but I
will always be the one
to Love You.

Magic and Lust

To talk of things that lead to a kiss ...
Mere simple words, magic and lust
a spark of something gold between us, scarlet flush
... words now ...
hushed. Mean more,
more
Quiet to all
a scream to you. You hear me, my love,
as I shout across time.
To talk, yes, of things ... things that lead to a kiss.
Whispers. Secrets.
Unsure in the dark, be not afraid to speak.
The heat of our voices,
not air, not smoke, not fog,
impossible to vanish.
Fire, open mouths.
Eyes, golden light.
Two souls ... burning.
Wait. And Listen. Once more
for my voice. To kiss.
Kiss with magic and lust.

Dawn

Who is this frightened girl
with bright face covered in night?
a little wisp of smoke seeping out of a corner
the last ember flickers
But wait!
She saw Me,
crimson
waiting ...
One bit of friction
Spark!
red-gold-then-orange
endlessly aflame
returning
illuminated liberated
from darkness.

Over and over
again
She will see Me.
The eternal hearth
unstoppable love
to ignite and consume
Her!
I do not set.
I do not rise.
I am always There
bringing Her! warmth
bringing Her! light.

About the author

Michelle Cushing is the contemporary Southern writer of the novels *From a Vine* (2007), *Faith Orion's Field* (2008), and *Rosabelle, believe* (2010), all published by Mulberry Bark. After receiving a degree from the prestigious journalism department of the University of Arkansas and graduating magna cum laude, she published several articles and began collaborating on screenplays with her sister, writer/director Christie XT Cushing (*The Mask of Aubrey Clover*). She co-produced and starred in the 2010 Cannes Film Festival "Short Film Corner" Official Selection, *Scars at the Spook House*. She is part Cherokee and a distant relative to both Peter Cushing and John Wayne. Her writing influences include Tennessee Williams, Richard Bach, and Eudora Welty.

www.ingramcontent.com/pod-product-compliance
Lightning Source LLC
Chambersburg PA
CBHW061616100726
47898CB00002B/680